KONTAKTE AND OTHER STORIES

KONTAKTE AND OTHER STORIES

Jonathan Taylor

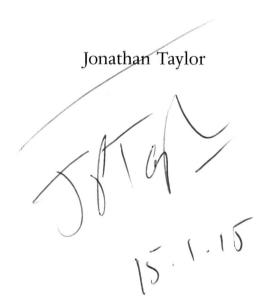

15 . 1 . 15

ROMAN *Books*
www.roman-books.co.uk

Copyright © 2013 Jonathan Taylor

ISBN 978-93-80905-70-9

Typeset in Dante MT Std

First published 2013
This edition published 2014

1 3 5 7 9 8 6 4 2

British Library Cataloguing in Publication Data.
A catalogue record for this book is available from the British Library.

Publisher: Suman Chakraborty

ROMAN Books
26 York Street, London W1U 6PZ, United Kingdom
Unit 49, Park Plaza, South Block, Ground Floor, 71, Park Street, Kolkata 700016, WB, India
2nd Floor, 38/3, Andul Road, Howrah 711109, WB, India
www.roman-books.co.uk | www.romanbooks.co.in

Printed and bound in India by
Repro India Ltd

It's as if someone were beating you with a stick and saying, 'Your business is rejoicing,' and you rise, shakily, and go marching off muttering, 'Our business is rejoicing, our business is rejoicing.'

Dmitri Shostakovich and Solomon Volkov, *Testimony*

Versions of the following stories have been previously published in *The Aesthetica*, *Blue-Eyed Boybait Magazine*, *A Chide's Alphabet*, *Coffee House Magazine*, *Connotation Press: An Online Artifact*, *Litro Magazine*, *Necessary Fiction*, *Overheard: Stories to Read Aloud* (Salt, 2012), *Raw Edge Magazine*, *Stand Magazine*, *Staple Magazine*, *Veto Magazine* and *The Warwick Review*.

For John Schad

Contents

Preface
On Musical Fictions

All art constantly aspires to the condition of music.
— Walter Pater, *The Renaissance*

Over the last 250 years, thousands of short stories, novellas and novels have explored musical themes, or revolved around musical characters. The late-eighteenth and nineteenth centuries, particularly, are full of such stories and characters. Wackenroder's 'Joseph Berlinger,' Hoffmann's tales, Poe's fiction, Balzac's musician *Gambara*, Dickens's *The Mystery of Edwin Drood*, Hardy's stories, Du Maurier's *Trilby*, Leo Tolstoy's *Kreutzer Sonata*, all include musical images, themes and characters. No doubt this literary fascination with music and the figure of the musician originates in their Romantic elevation to the highest spiritual realms by philosophers like Schopenhauer and Pater, and real-life musicians like Richard Wagner. As Friedrich Nietzsche writes in *On the Genealogy of Morals*:

> With this extraordinary inflation in the value of music, which seemed to follow from Schopenhauer's philosophy, the musician too suddenly rose in value: from that moment on

he became an oracle, a priest, even more than a priest, a sort of spokesman of the 'in itself' of things ... From that time on he ceased to talk just music, this ventriloquist of God—he talked metaphysics.

Some things have changed since Nietzsche wrote this in 1887, but the fascination in fiction with music and musicians remains. There are numerous twentieth- and twenty-first-century authors who write about music and musicians—from Thomas Mann and Anthony Burgess, to Roddy Doyle, Rose Tremain, and Nick Hornby; there are whole anthologies of stories about music, such as those edited by Peter Wild, and inspired by The Smiths and The Fall; there is even a publisher in New York, Coral Press, which specializes in publishing 'musical fiction'.

There is arguably a difference, though, between earlier and later portrayals of musicians in fiction: Thomas Mann's composer in *Doctor Faustus* cuts a very different figure to some of the more idealized portrayals of musicians in the high-Romantic era. Wagner's posthumous association with Hitler and Nazism, coupled with his own egotism and avowed anti-Semitism, have inevitably had their effects on later fictional musicians. Arguably, one such effect is a disillusioned, and partly self-conscious, turning away from perceived Romantic 'high' cultural models of music and the musician—so that many writers of the later twentieth century preferred to focus on 'popular' music and musicians of one kind or another.

Of course, this survey is all rather generalized, and history never quite works in such a linear way. The emphasis on popular culture, and the corresponding suspicion of musicians and musical power, was actually with us long before—in the nineteenth-century fiction of Poe, Balzac, Du Maurier, and Hardy. Conversely, the later twentieth- and twenty-first centuries have not entirely turned away from earlier idealizations of music; Vikram Seth's beautiful writing on music, for example, owes a great deal to Romantic conceptions, translating Schubert's or Bach's music into the rather blunter medium of the English language.

Many fiction writers have attempted this—to write musical fiction which is not merely about music, but which somehow echoes that music within the constraints of written prose. This is the kind of musical fiction which interests me—fiction which is not just musically themed, but which, in its style, its punctuation, its cadences and its imagery, attempts to capture the strange and elusive narratives of music; and not just any music, or music in general, but the particular music with which the fiction is concerned—whether that music is Stockhausen or The Smiths, Puccini or Piaf.

Short stories, I think, are particularly good at this, partly because the time taken to read a short story is often similar to the time taken to listen to a piece of music; one can mirror the narrative structure of the other quite closely. The very compression and intensity of short fiction means that it lends itself more readily to the portrayal and simulation of the compressed intensity of musical works.

In stylistically simulating musical techniques, fiction often comes very close to poetry, which, after all, self-consciously uses musical elements of language as part of its repertoire. Like poetry, musical fiction will often use alliteration, assonance, onomatopoeia, rhythm, allusion, refrains, even rhyme, to simulate the music it is describing. And the more like poetry it becomes, the more musical fiction inevitably starts to bend and then break some of the basic 'rules' of prose, such as conventional uses of grammar, punctuation, lineation and paragraphing. To attempt to describe music, to encapsulate its fluid structures and timbres, it would often seem necessary to write in a more fluid, flexible, poetic way;

and examples of this kind of poetic prose abound in musical fiction.

However weak we may feel that words are in comparison to music, many composers have struggled in the opposite direction to that of writers, attempting to connect their art form with written language. Schubert's songs, Wagner's *Gesamtskunstwerk*, Berlioz's, Liszt's and Strauss's tone poems and other programmatic works—all appropriate written narratives and texts, and, in their very different ways, attempt to shape these narratives and texts into music. This act of shaping material from words into music had—and maybe still has—the same kind of distorting effects on musical language as the reverse has on written language. The nineteenth- and early twentieth-century composers most credited with writing music informed by written texts are the same composers who are usually credited with stretching, bending and sometimes even breaking conventional musical language. It would seem that the very attempt to cross between different art forms necessarily distorts, bends, breaks and transforms the languages of those art forms. But then, I believe that this is precisely what artists of all kinds—whether musicians, short-story writers, novelists or poets—should be attempting to do: challenging, subverting and reinventing the conventional languages of their chosen art forms.

A version of this Preface was originally published on Thresholds: International Short Story Forum, *2013. The quotation from Nietzsche is in* The Genealogy of Morals, *trans. Douglas Smith, Oxford: Oxford University Press, 2008, p.83.*

O Terra, Addio

They've been locked in for half an hour, sitting on top of one of the exhibits. It's dark except for the pyramidical outlines of the lasers they are trapped between. It's silent except for rain against the barred window high up on one wall, just above pavement level. It's still apart from the tapping of fingers on glass or stilettos on an explanatory plaque:

Sarcophagus and mummy of High Priest Nesperennub of Karnak, Temple of Amun, late New Kingdom, c.1100 BC. On loan from the British Museum. Display also includes copy of Nesperennub's Book of the Dead, scarabs, head-dresses, tyet amulets, shabti figurines, etc. The sarcophagus is decorated with gold and displays common funerary motifs. These include the scene of judgement in which Nesperennub's heart is weighed against the feather of truth.

Serena had been on the way to a fund-raiser for the museum when it happened. 'Why don't you go down and speak to the Prof. while I finish off here?' her husband had suggested through his secretary's intercom. 'Be down in a bit.'

She'd stamped her foot and pouted: 'No, no, no, no. I'm not going to be all nicey-nice to someone you and your cronies're

17

about to chop,' and she'd stormed out of the office, declaring her intention to go straight to the gala on her own. Oops. First mistake.

On the way downstairs, she'd had second thoughts, and skipped down the extra flight to look in on the Professor after all. Second thoughts, second mistake.

The Prof. was in the back office, working on some papyri documents—documents he was still working on, mentally speaking, when he offered to make Serena a cup of tea and tried to make small talk.

'How are you?'

'Amazing. Amazing.'

'Really?'

'No, yes, no. I mean, these papers are amazing. They're about Amenhotep's heresy. You know the one—fourteenth century?' She didn't, but nodded anyway and made *him* a cup of tea. He continued waving his mug around and effusing about Amenhotep.

The cup of tea was the third mistake. The Egyptology department could only afford a suitably ancient kettle which shrieked, so they hadn't heard the security guard's final, 'No one here?' from the exhibition room.

They'd just heard the locking up …

…at which point, they'd dropped the mugs, turned, and run like a pair of middle-aged Indiana Joneses—one sliding in his slippers, the other click-clacking in stilettos—trying to get out of a booby-trapped chamber. Too late; and they'd suddenly frozen, surrounded by laser beams. A few inches in any direction and the alarms would have been activated.

'This has never happened to me before, never,' whined the Professor. 'It's that company they've farmed security out to. I s'pose we could set the alarms off and attract attention that way?' As someone used to acknowledging every side of an argument, however trivial, he added, 'But then, well, the ensuing fuss might cost the museum a lot of money. You know, police, extra security guards and all that. And, well, we don't want to get shot or anything drastic.'

It was she who decided the issue with a definite: 'No, let's wait. Let's see how long it takes my husband to miss us. Me ... us.'

Half an hour passes. Serena's humming a melody in a perfectly pitched soprano. Locked together in the darkening exhibition room with a storm beating against the window, trapped between interlocking laser beams and the glass-encased sarcophagus of Priest Nesperennub of Karnak, the Professor feels a claustrophobia of femininity—a claustrophobia which is filling the space around him. If he looks up at the window, he has to look past the top of her dress and the Cleopatra-ish whiteness of her breasts; if he looks down at the floor tiles, he has to look past the curve of her nylon-clad calves; if he shuts his eyes, he can hear her strange song; if he breathes in, he inhales waves of expensive perfume (rather better, it strikes him, than the melted fat used by pharaonic concubines); if he remains absolutely still, he's sure he can feel the minute hairs on her left arm touching the minute hairs on his—in such a restricted space, this is as close to not being close that they can possibly get.

And he's worried. He's worried that this claustrophobia of femininity is causing another kind of claustrophobia—a claustrophobia in his trousers—and that she might notice. Although he gets on okay with his friend's wife, he hardly knows her well enough for such an embarrassment to be a joke. He doesn't know *any* woman well enough for that.

Having perched with the Prof. on top of Priest Nesperennub for some time, Serena gets up and stretches her legs, shaking her brown hair loose. She feels a little peculiar sitting on the glass case, with the 3,000-year-old High Priest of Karnak staring up at her bottom ('Does it look big in this, Nesperennub, dear?'). The actual mummy is shut in the sarcophagus, but she can't help remembering something the Prof. had told her years before—that the sarcophagi have two holes drilled in the face mask, so the corpse can see what's going on outside. At the time, she'd laughed and said it reminded her of the portraits with moving eyes in *Scooby Doo* cartoons. Now, locked in this semi-darkness with the dead, the analogy doesn't seem quite so funny.

'I feel like Aïda, buried alive down here.'

'What's an "Aïda"?'

'Professor, you are funny. How come you, of all people, don't know that?'

She continues humming, the tune gradually and quietly evolving into words: '*Presago il core della tua condanna, in questa tomba che per te s'apriva...*'

'What does that mean?' asks the Prof. 'My modern Italian isn't up to my Ancient Egyptian.'

She doesn't answer, and instead turns round to face him, her bosom pressing lightly against his knees. He tries his best not to break eye contact, concerned that everything—even *not* looking down at her chest—might betray what's on his mind. She's bound to notice, he thinks, that I'm deliberately trying not to glance at her breasts; she's bound to work out that what not staring really means is not-not staring. After all, in the many years I've known her, this must be the first time I've ever established eye contact with her, instead of poring over hieroglyphs or mural fragments. And now I am looking at her, I see those murals in her: her eye make-up reminds me of the women on the mural of Ramses III's harem; her breasts (which I am not looking at) are those of Rixen's Cleopatra.

'You do know that my husband is shutting your department?'

He stammers, knowing he's trapped with awkward questions. 'I'd... I'd guessed as much.'

'Doesn't that make you angry—a so-called friend of twenty years closing you down, a friend you studied with, came to the museum with?'

'I've been here a long while, Mrs Usher. The museum isn't getting any richer.'

'That sounds like *him* talking. First the museum sends you down here and "streamlines" your staff. Now it's streamlining you out of existence.'

'To be fair, we don't get many visitors. Not like the Technology department. There just aren't enough buttons to press in Egypt, I suppose. You can't have interactive mummies.' He sighs. 'Not that the children mind. They love the stuff about embalming and death. It's the parents who get bored.'

She looks askance at him, but he doesn't seem to be joking. 'He never jokes, never gets jokes,' she remembers her husband complaining, following an abortive tour of the Egyptology department with one of the museum's industrial sponsors. 'He has all the social skills of his precious Osiris.' Unlike her soon-to-be-knighted husband, that is.

'Again, to be fair, I can see that we're out of date. Three thousand years out of date. It's not your husband, Mrs Usher, to blame. It's us, Nesperennub and me. To be fair.'

'For God's or Osiris's or whoever's sake, stop saying "to be fair"!' She stamps her foot for the umpteenth time today. 'Don't you feel something about *anything*? There must be more to the mummy than bandages—more to your feelings than "to be fair"?' Always operatic, she's holding her hands in the air as if shaking him.

And, when he speaks—quietly, methodically—it seems she's

shaken him into passion from a millennia-long sleep: 'Did you know that, in 1976, the French laid on a guard of honour, a brass band, a red carpet to receive the mummy of Ramses the Second? They put on a state welcome at Orly Airport for a king who'd been dead for over three thousand years—did you know that? And now look, look what we're reduced to'—in his 'we', he indicates with a sweep of his hand the mummies, the figurines, the statues of Amun-Ra, and the murals of Sobek and Seth as his companions in bankruptcy—'an underground vault no one visits, and soon a lumber room. Perhaps in hundreds of years' time, a new Howard Carter will rediscover me and my department.' He swallows a deep breath. 'I'm sorry, Mrs Usher, I'm sorry, but your husband's become our "Ammut the Devourer" when he was meant to be my friend. I didn't have any others.'

He repeats 'I'm sorry,' but she's not offended. Instead, she sits next to him again on the glass case. She places her manicured fingers on his knee and then takes them off again and then puts them on again. From upstairs, they can hear the distant tramp-tramp-tramp of a security guard. The Professor's heart is beating quickly, his breathing is shallow; he doesn't know why. 'Security'll find us soon enough.' They're not looking at each other now: she's staring at the ceiling, in the direction of the tramp-tramp-tramp, he at the floor, past her thighs, past her calves, past her stilettoed feet.

The hum that's turning into a song comes from a long way away, a long time ago and, for a moment, the Professor thinks it's in his head. While she's singing, her hand tightens slightly on his knee, stroking upwards and downwards to the rhythm. He feels sure that she doesn't know she's doing it, however aware of the touch he is.

'*Presago il core della tua condanna, in questa tomba che per te s'apriva io penetrai furtiva … E qui lontana da ogni umano sguardo nelle tue braccia desiai morire …'*

'What does that mean?'

She sings the answer, sketching out the same tune beneath an awkward translation: 'My heart had told me the fate that you were to suffer. Secretly, I found this tomb, that was soon to receive you, and, far from every human eye, in your arms I have chosen to die.'

'It's beautiful,' he whispers. 'What is it?'

'*Aïda.*'

'So, again, what is this *Aïda*?'

'A nineteenth-century Italian opera. By Verdi. You must have heard of him?'

'I don't get out of Ancient Egypt much.'

'But this is set in Egypt. In Memphis. It was premiered in Cairo.' Serena blushes. 'I … I know because I played the heroine in an am-dram production of it last year. A rather long-in-the-tooth Aïda, but…' There's no prompting flattery from the Professor, so she continues: '*Aïda* is everything I know of Egyptian history.'

'Doesn't bring to mind any Egyptian history I'm aware of. And I know most of it.'

'They said it was based on a story by someone called Auguste Mariette.'

The Prof. snorts: 'Oh, that Indiana Jones vandal. No doubt it was made up, then.'

Cut short, the conversation is replaced by silence and rain. Her singing and her stroking have stopped. The Professor tries to think of something to say to make up for his abruptness, to restart the stalled motion of her hand. He's not used to having to interact with someone born after Christ. 'Erm. Yes, Mariette. You know, he's also the one who discovered one of our pieces here. That fragment over there from the Serapaeum, of the mummified bull.'

'Why on earth would they mummify bulls?'

'Why? Because bulls were meant to be embodiments of the god Ptah.'

'Ptah features in the opera too, you know.' Her hand is moving gently once more, her operatic trance returning. 'It's Ptah whom the priests and priestesses invoke in their sentence on Radamès. They're chanting offstage: *Immenso, Immenso Fthà, del mondo spirito animator.*' Upstairs, the tramp-tramp-tramp of the security guard has stopped for a moment and there's an exchange of voices, deepened by the distance. The tramp-tramp-tramp starts again. Serena slips from speaking to singing and back again, as though two voices, one ancient, one modern, one stylized Ethiopian princess, one sophisticated society lady, co-exist in her: 'But I don't remember any bulls being mentioned.'

'I'm lost: who's Radamès?'

'He's the hero. It's the final scene of the opera, and he's been sentenced to being buried alive—being shut in his tomb for treason. That's why I'm like Aïda here. Aïda with lasers.'

'What's Aïda got to do with it?' What with the singing and stroking, he hardly knows what he's saying, how he's managing to maintain a conversation; maybe, like her, he is a composite of two beings, one conscious Egyptologist, one mass of urges, one *lector* who speaks, one *ka* who desires.

'Aïda's in love with Radamès—and his treason is that he, an Egyptian warrior, loves her, an Ethiopian princess, back. In that last scene, she suddenly appears to Radamès: *Son io!*' Gripping his knee, Serena opens her voice and belts the phrase at full volume, as if shouting operatically for help. He realizes that calling for help, operatically or otherwise, is something neither of them have even thought of doing. He wonders why, not quite guessing that his long-buried *ka* might be colluding with her underground Aïda, and that both *ka* and Aïda understand what's going on far better than their conscious selves—that *ka* and Aïda might have decided what was going to happen a long time before.

'Aïda's hidden away in the tomb beforehand, so they can die there together, arm in arm, voice in voice.'

Arm in arm, voice in voice: at these words, the Professor wants to reciprocate Serena's hold on his knee so much, his hand touching the thigh which is exposed by her dress riding up. Instead, his above-ground self mutters: 'That sounds ghastly. And certainly not based on historical fact.'

'History isn't everything. Not for them, anyway. And it's not ghastly, or not *just* ghastly.' In this quiet, in this stillness, she explains by singing, her half-voice soprano infused with a G flat major ghastliness and loveliness she couldn't sustain on stage: '*Vedi? Di morte l'angelo radiante a noi s'appressa; ne adduce a eterni gaudii sovra i suoi vanni d'ôr.*' The Professor feels he is somehow excavating long-forgotten music, as if her melody has been going on beneath the earth—quieter and quieter, turning to stone—for three thousand years.

'What does that mean?' he asks, leaning towards her as he might put his head against the earth to listen. *Sing, keep singing.* His hand is on her thigh and his speaking self hasn't even realized yet.

'It means...' and she echoes the tune again, extending it at the end into a delicate cadenza, 'See? The angel of death radiantly approaches us, to take us to eternal joys on its wings of gold.'

Serena's face is only a couple of inches away from the Professor's now. She's singing straight ahead, but his whole body is turned towards her, musically charmed into contortion like a *kherep Selket*'s snake. Upstairs, there are steps and voices again, deep and urgent. 'They'll find us,' she whispers. 'That's my husband's drone, I'm sure.'

He realizes now that his hand is on her nylon leg and he gasps, 'Sing some more.'

She takes a shaky breath: 'They sing together, Aïda and Radamès—so… so let's do the same. It goes like this. *O terra, addio; addio, valle di pianti … Sogno di gaudio che in dolor svanì. A noi si schiude il ciel e l'alme erranti volano al raggio dell'eterno dì.* O farewell, earth; farewell, vale of tears… dream of joy that has vanished into sorrow. The heavens welcome our errant souls, and we fly towards eternal day.' She pauses. 'Go on. No one's here. No one can hear but me and you and good old Nesperennub.' Breathing in her perfume, he follows her musical line with a tenor-ish voice which hasn't been infused with melody for decades, but which at least rises and falls with hers: '*O terra, addio; addio, valle di pianti … Sogno di gaudio che in dolor svanì. A noi si schiude il ciel e l'alme erranti volano al raggio dell'eterno dì.*'

She's still not looking at his face, however close it is, but nor has she moved his hand from her thigh: 'And they keep repeating this over and again, and the priests and priestesses keep chanting *Immenso Fthà*, and the Egyptian princess, who had also loved Radamès and who'd wanted him for herself, sings *Isi placata ti schiuda il ciel!*—Isis shall grant you eternal rest! You see, she's locked out of the tomb forever, just as they're locked in. Both tragedies are just as bad as each other.'

Serena and the Professor aren't going to be locked in by the lasers forever, and nor are those outside going to stay shut out; there are hurried footsteps upstairs. The phone rings in the Professor's office.

The two of them don't hear and can't move from where they are anyway … and his hand is tremblingly moving higher and higher up her thigh and he wants to sing the duet again and his face is an inch from her cheek and he feels terribly out of breath and ... and he doesn't care about historical inaccuracies any more.

'They're buried alive, but they keep singing this infinite lullaby. *Ah! Si schiude il ciel. O terra addio, addio valle di pianti.'*

There are footsteps running up and down the stairs. The phone keeps ringing. In a distant part of the building, the alarm has been set off after all. The Professor's fingers have found the bare place above her stockings; he can't remember the last time he touched living skin. He thinks she'll stop him, slap him, shout for help any moment ... but no. She leans back and his unpractised fingers circle up and up and up.

'Sogno di gaudio che in dolor svanì. A noi si schiude il ciel, si schiude il ciel e l'alme erranti...'

His fingers find her underwear.

For a moment, she stops him, pushes his hand away, and he waits for the opera to end with a slap. Instead, she pulls up her dress and then puts his hand back where it was. She even manages to giggle—between soprano gasps—and whisper that she hopes the High Priest of Karnak is enjoying what he can see through his *Scooby Doo* eyes. A curious ménage à trois, thinks the bewildered Professor.

'Volano al raggio dell'eterno dì, il ciel, il ciel, si schiude il ciel, si schiude il ciel.' Someone's run downstairs now and is pounding at the door. 'Open this door!' It's the voice of her husband, his friend. 'Get this door open now.' Other footsteps run down the stairs. 'Are you in there, Serena?'

She can't answer, and she's arching her back, stretched over the cabinet, and the beautiful soprano voice is punctuated by intakes of breath and...

'Volano al raggio dell'eterno dì, il ciel, il ciel, si schiude il ciel, si schiude il ciel.'

Far away in a tomb which never existed, long ago in a history that never happened, in a story which was made up, Aïda is still singing and falling and dying, arm in arm, voice in voice with Radamès.

The doors are unlocked and a torch finds them.

Finds them standing up, stretching their legs, smoothing down their clothes—no doubt, relieved to be rescued. No doubt. Their rescuer is squinting through the darkness: 'Why didn't you set the alarms off? Come on, we're late for this dinner. It's important, you know.'

And they follow him out of the Egyptology department, away from Nesperennub, away from history, away from *faux* history, and away from Aïda and Radamès, on whom the door slams shut.

'Ladies and Gentlemen, Tonight's Concert Will Commence in Fifteen Minutes'

But she remains sitting.

She remains sitting in the bar area.

She remains sitting in the bar area of the Victoria Hall, Hanley, sipping her usual.

She remains sitting in the bar area of the Victoria Hall, sipping her usual, waiting for Charlie.

She remains sitting in the bar area of the Victoria Hall, sipping her usual, waiting for Charlie and Tchaikovsky.

She knows what has happened.

She knows what has happened to Charlie's wife.

She knows what has happened to Charlie's wife, since their last concert, a month ago.

She knows what has happened to Charlie's wife, since their last concert, a month ago—the cancer, the funeral, the notices in the *Evening Sentinel*.

Despite that, she knows he will come through that door in a minute or two.

She knows he will come through that door in a minute or two, kiss her hand, take her arm and lead her through Door B to the stalls.

She knows he will come through that door in a minute or two, kiss her hand, take her arm and lead her through Door B to the stalls, as he has done for the last nineteen years. After nineteen years, she no longer needs him—and he probably no longer dares—to call in advance, to arrange their meetings. All she needs to do, every September, is just get hold of the Victoria Hall's calendar for the season, and pencil all the Tchaikovsky concerts into her diary—because she knows that, on those evenings, he will come through that door, kiss her hand, feign surprise at their accidental meeting, and lead her through Door B to the stalls.

Or, at least, she used to know that, used to be sure.

But this particular evening she also dreads something else.

She also dreads that he will come through the door ... differently.

She dreads that he will stride through the door differently, with a new mac, a bunch of chrysanths, a new kind of assurance.

She dreads that he will come through the door differently, with a new mac, a bunch of chrysanths, a new kind of assurance, and sit next to her and say: 'Now she's gone, let's not do the concert this time. Now she's gone, let's change nineteen years of habit. Now she's gone, let's talk, sit, walk, kiss, go on holiday, get married, all to the music of Tchaikovsky. I loved *her*, but she's gone. Now I can love you instead. I've known you for nineteen years. Nineteen long years.'

And after nineteen long years, she'll have to tell him.

After nineteen years, she'll have to tell him that, for her, it's still a business arrangement. Still a matter of £60. Nothing more nor less. Honestly, nothing else at all, whatsoever, in the slightest, even after nineteen years. The music was neither here nor there, even after nineteen years.

Even after nineteen years.

Nineteen years—two more years than he was married to *her*.

Ladies and gentlemen, tonight's concert will commence in ten minutes.

He was lonely.

He was lonely back then.

He was lonely back then, and he'd found her classified ad and dialled the number.

He was lonely back then, and he'd found her classified ad and dialled the number: 'Do you like Tchaikovsky?' he'd asked.

It was an unusual pick-up line, and she'd been tempted to reply with something like, 'What position is that?' or 'Is that something the Slavic ones do?'

But she hadn't; she had lied instead: 'Yes, of course, everyone likes him; great stuff, love it,' and that had been that, for nineteen years. Nineteen years of Tchaikovsky. Nineteen years of deafening Russian brass, self-indulgent emotionalism, tunes that spun round and round her head for days afterwards, didn't stop even while she was faking orgasms with other clients. Nineteen years of waiting for him here, sipping her usual, being led through Door B to the stalls, sitting on bum-numbing chairs, pretending not to be bored or near sleep, now and then squeezing his knee, now and then catching his eye moving down her blouse, or up her thigh towards a strategically exposed stocking-top, now and then glancing at him when he wasn't looking, when he was engrossed in some particularly intense *fortissimo* moment—at his side-combed hair, his dandruff, his bony shoulders—and thinking, for that moment, the music had done something to his eyes, made them seem too droopy-heavy for his face, or somehow too heavy for her, and she'd look away again, thinking instead of the £20,

£30, £40 or £50, depending on inflation, which she would get at the end of the night, and which would pay for something she thought she needed.

Ladies and gentlemen, tonight's concert will commence in five minutes. Please take your seats.

She'd thought all this would finish when he met *her*.

She'd thought it would finish when he met *her*, when he married *her*.

She'd thought it would finish when he met *her*, when he married *her*, when she started the new accounts job, when she got married herself, didn't have a kid, then got divorced, when gradually, one by one, her old regulars—all of whom preferred, shall we say, non-Tchaikovskyian services—stopped calling.

'You don't need me any more,' she'd said to him, one 1812 evening. 'Why don't you bring *her* instead?'

'She doesn't like Tchaikovsky. She likes Michael Barrymore.'

'Oh.'

'She thinks I come on my own. Or, at least, I think she thinks that.'

'Oh.'

'No one here knows either my wife or me—well, apart from you. I think.'

'Oh.'

And so it carried on.

And so the concerti, the overtures, the ballet excerpts, the eardrum-thumping symphonies carried on.

Ladies and gentlemen, tonight's concert is about to begin. Please take your seats.

And so the concerti, the overtures, the ballet excerpts, the symphonies carried on, till now.

But now he is not here.

She glances over at the upside-down programme clutched by a couple rushing past her, reading the words right to left: *ynohpmyS euqitéhtaP, yksvokiahcT*. She doesn't need to reverse the words. She knows already she's in the right place at the right time.

But he is not.

He is not here.

He is not here, and there is quiet around her.

He is not here, and there is quiet around her, a hush in the concert hall.

He is not here, and there is quiet around her, a hush in the concert hall, followed by applause for leader and conductor.

He is not here, and there is quiet around her, a hush in the concert hall, followed by applause for leader and conductor—and then, Tchaikovsky's *Pathétique*, his favourite, is creeping, on *pianissimo* bassoon, through the half-open door to the stalls opposite.

Tchaikovsky's *Pathétique*, his favourite, is creeping, on *pianissimo* bassoon, through the half-open door to the stalls opposite: first movement, *Allegro non troppo*, then second movement, *Allegro con grazia*, then *Allegro molto vivace*, and finally,

and finally, sitting alone with her empty glass, only the *Adagio lamentoso* filling it, she thinks of Charlie's side-combed hair, his dandruff, his bony shoulders,

and finally, sitting alone with her empty glass and only the *Adagio lamentoso* filling it, she thinks about what this music, which she has heard so many times before, but never *really* heard, seemed to do to his eyes, making them too droopy heavy for his face, making them too heavy for her, making her look away.

Or, at least, until now.

At least until now, when she no longer wants to look away.

At least until now, as the gong, the bassoon, the final B minor

33

chords, make even her ageing eyes feel too droopy-heavy for this
world and
 and she pushes her glass away,
 and leaves before the applause.

Kontakte

Derek came in from the cold and sat on the bed.

Derek got up from the bed and went to make a coffee.

Derek gave up making a coffee and sat back on the bed.

The kettle boiled, unregarded.

Derek sat in the dark.

Derek got up again and stepped over to the stereo. He pressed 'play' on the tape recorder. He sat back on the bed.

In the dark, on the bed, Derek was surrounded by Karlheinz Stockhausen's electronic music.

There were pings, crunches and strangely comic doings.

One of the neighbours may or may not have banged on the wall to tell Derek to shut his Stockhausen up. He couldn't be sure whether it was the neighbour or the tape.

Derek sat in the dark on the bed.

The kettle boiled dry and faded into the music.

The tape ended.

Derek was going to get up, but didn't.

The tape automatically rewound itself and started again.

Derek sat in the dark.

The tape finished a second time, rewound itself and started again.

Derek sat in the dark.

After a few hours, things started to lunge out of the music at him.

After a few hours, he thought he heard the dog from upstairs woofing amongst the white noise.

After another hour, he thought he heard the ducks in Acton Park. Stockhausen ducks.

Derek sat in the dark.

There were whispers from hell.

There were cars and lorries and the teleport in *Star Trek* and yesterday's indigestion.

Then there was his mother's voice on the crackly line from Australia, telling him to keep away from 'that bobble-hat girl'.

Then there was his own voice telling 'that bobble-hat girl' to keep away from him, her asking why, and he arguing back, telling her it didn't matter how old he was, how old she was, how much he liked spotting her bobble hat from the Uxbridge Road, how far away his mother was, and so on and so forth: the fact was that feeding ducks together in Acton Park was no basis for a long-term relationship, since his mother didn't approve of ducks, Acton, parks, bobble hats, the Uxbridge Road, and any combination thereof. 'You're better off sticking to your tapes,' the crackly voice said from Down Under, 'than gallivanting round feeding ducks with all and sundry.'

Derek sat in the dark, sticking with his tapes.

After another few hours, it was trying to get light outside the curtains.

The music just sounded like white noise again.

Derek got up from the bed. He had a bit of a headache.

He walked over to the stereo.

He pressed the 'stop' button.

The 'stop' button was jammed.

He pressed it again.

It didn't budge.

The tape rewound itself.

Derek stood for a moment, wondering what to do, shifting his weight from one foot to the other.

Stockhausen started again.

Derek sighed and sat back down on the bed.

Must Sound Genuine

Their works are marked by formalist perversions, anti-democratic tendencies which are alien to the Soviet people and their artistic tastes.

(Central Committee, Decree on Music, 1948)

Long into the night, the composer sits at his piano, sketching out a new symphony.

For this new symphony, the composer is using words, not notes.

The composer is trying to believe—genuinely believe—that this is because he has transcended notes, exchanging them for concepts.

The composer is trying not to believe the opposite, that he has been mugged, defrauded, pick-pocketed, fleeced of notes—just as, thirteen months before, he was robbed of his contralto wife—till all he has left are these amusical words:

Sketch for a Soviet Symphony in One Movement, to be dedicated to Andrei Alexandrovich Zhdanov, Chairman of the RSFSR Supreme Soviet.

Opening, Fig. 1: 6/8 Adagio, C Minor, pianissimo possibile rising
to pianissimo, and gradually to piano: low strings, contra-bassoon,
symbolizing Tsarist regime; tetratones protesting on Bb clarinets,
symbolizing oppressed proletariat...

...or perhaps not tetratones: that might sound too dissonant, too
much like he is revelling in discords, too—God save him—
bourgeois-formalist. Even worse, it might sound like he was
associating the progressive forces of proletarian defiance with
Western modernism. *Govno.* Shit.

Okay, okay. Perhaps instead the clarinets should play in unison
(or doubled at the octave), echoing the clarinets in Tchaikovsky's
Fifth.

Yes, the composer thinks, echoing Tchaikovsky's Fifth couldn't
possibly sound formalist or bourgeois or discordant. And members
of the Central Committee and the new guys at the Union of
Composers, Khrennikov and his henchmen, they all like
Tchaikovsky. Everyone likes Tchaikovsky.

Except that ... well, except that ... what if it all sounds
too Tchaikovskyian, too familiar? What if the protests of the
proletariat seem too soft, too muted, too Tsarist? It might sound
like he's associating Socialist progressivism with retrogressive
Tsarism. *Govno.* Shit.

Or perhaps...

Or perhaps, the composer thinks, he should forget about the
musical details for now. Let's not worry about what the clarinets
are actually playing. Let's concentrate on the conceptual 'shape'
of the piece. The notes will take care of themselves. The notes
come later.

Surely the notes will come later.

In the meantime, there are still words to scribble down:

Fig 2: 3/4 Andante Cantabile: melismatic F minor solo for cor anglais, above swirling deep cellos and double basses, the melody (which must be heartfelt, truthful) symbolizing the repressed work-er's pain under capitalism, the aching worker's heart, his misplaced striving, individualistic yearning, his consciousness still false, yet to shake off his chains, yet to unite with others in glorious uprising...

Good, good, thinks the composer, almost crying, this might just work. Please, God, after everything you've put me through the last thirteen months, after that last row, the aborted premiere, the loneliness, the silent phone calls at night, the endless whisper-whisper-whispering, the space in my scores where her contralto should have been—please let it work.

After all, it—or something like it—worked in '33 for Dmitri. In '33, Dmitri came back to life after all that chaos-not-music horror in *Pravda*. Dmitri came back with his Fifth Symphony, his 'Artist's Creative Response to Just Criticism'. So rehabilitation was possible. It was. Is.

Although...

Although there was always something that bothered the composer in those endlessly repeated *A*s in the finale of Dmitri's Fifth. Something not quite right. Not quite ... sincere. Or perhaps it was something wrong with his own hearing. Perhaps the music *was* sincere, and it was his hearing which was corrupted. Too much Second Viennese School taken when young. Too much insincere Western poison poured into his ears, to the point that he could no longer separate the sincere from the insincere, Socialist reality from capitalist *khuinya*—bollocks.

Still, no one else seemed to have had that problem with Dmitri's Fifth. No one else—or no *apparatchik* of consequence—seemed to have noticed anything insincere about it, and Dmitri had survived. So why shouldn't the composer survive now, too?

And there are other ways to survive as well: there's that cowardly bastard Kabalevsky, who may or may not have knocked himself off The List by substituting someone else. Why shouldn't he do something like that through this symphony? Why shouldn't this symphony get him off The List? No, more: why shouldn't this new symphony take the Conservatory by storm, win him the Stalin Prize, make everyone, even him, happy? Why shouldn't this be the Perfect Soviet Symphony—the one for which everyone, from the Supreme Soviet downwards, has been waiting?

Of course, of course, he can't quite get the Perfect Soviet Symphony's notes yet. Of course, the notes are difficult. But the concepts. The concepts are coming thick and fast now, and he scribbles on and on into the night, ever more feverishly. Must get it all down, he thinks, before it's too late. Then they'll see. Then they'll understand.

In this symphony, the composer thinks, I will be an Engineer of Souls:

Fig. 3: Poco a Poco Accelerando, snarling trombe con sordini unite with cellos, mf, in grinding crescendo of repression, as lone cor anglais is drowned out by painful dissonance...

...but the question is: how much dissonance?

How much dissonance is permitted?

How much dissonance will the Composers' Union let me have, the composer wonders? Is there going to be a percentage, a ration? A ratio of dissonance to consonance? Is there going to be a decree?

Oh please, thinks the composer, let there be a decree, so I can know.

What he does know is that something has to be overcome in the symphony for it to be truly heroic, epic, revolutionary. There has to be darkness, conflict, dissonance at the start, for that darkness, conflict, dissonance to be overcome. But there mustn't be *too much* darkness, conflict, dissonance. The music mustn't revel in its own dissonance. That would be decadent, Western, bourgeois.

But then again, thinks the composer, if the overcoming is to be heroic, the original conflict must be sufficient to make it so. For the inevitable, diatonic triumph of Bolshevism to sound sufficiently beautiful at the end, to feel like a real revolutionary achievement, there needs to be some kind of initiating ugliness beforehand.

But if the original ugliness is too dissonant, he will be accused of reactionary formalism.

But if the original conflict isn't dissonant enough, the heroism will seem lame, the Tsarist-capitalist enemy too likeable, the music nostalgic, counter-revolutionary.

But, then again, if...

But if...

Hedged in by never-ending 'but ifs', the composer's mind suddenly extricates itself, Houdini-like, from the present—and, before he remembers not to remember, that remembering is itself dangerous, he glimpses himself writing at this same piano, ten, twenty years ago. He glimpses himself writing music which it is dangerous just to recall, which has now been deported to a symphonic Gulag: the utilitarian pseudo-jazz of the *Proletkult* and early '20s, the Stakhonovite machine music of the Five-Year Plans, the dissonant neo-Romanticism of his puppet opera *The Brothers Karamazov* in the early '30s, the heroic-epic-folk-inflected-nationalism of the war, when music seemed so vital, when some of his songs for contralto and orchestra ('Shadow in the Garden', 'For the Love of Our Kolkhoz', 'My Yurodivy') were smuggled between Allies on microfilm... and then came the end of the war, and those strange little reviews turning up here and there, faintly praising his new works, while digging at his 'facile' talent, which—it seemed—was overly influenced by musical fashions at the expense of 'a genuine portrayal of the People's Reality' ... his wife's continual singing-whingeing about his 'weakness' ... and then the silence, the loneliness, until, finally, finally, all the fuss boiling over about Muradeli's pathetic new opera, followed by the Decree, the Conference, the terror...

And now this. Sitting at his piano in the night, staging his own *zhdanovshchina* in his head.

And then:

Fig. 4: 2/4 crescendo and hurtling accelerando, to Allegro Agitato, brutal [but obviously not too brutal] Scherzo: Bolshevik awakenings of freedom in heroic fifths on riotous horns, stalked by swirling tutti, attacked by repeated diminished sevenths: D major, A flat minor on strings and wind, accompanied by side drum, rat-a-tat-tat, trying to quell upsurge of revolutionary feeling...

...and those diminished sevenths with side drum must not, on any account, percussively remind him, or anyone else, of the knock-crack-knock on the door that night, thirteen and a half months ago, when the NKVD came for his wife.

No, the composer thinks, the composer wants to think, it is not for music to remember such things. Music, *our* music, should forget. Music should replay the past, only for it to be overcome. Music should strive onwards, forwards:

... to final fugato, eventually surmounted by fig. 5: 4/4 piccolos, flutes, oboes, Allegro non troppo, proclaiming the victory of October in emphatic triadic C major: wordless chorus, trumpets, trombones, organ, timpani,

    forte-fortissimo C major,
    trombonissimo C major,

molto pesante, molto pesante, molto pesante,
forte-fortissimo, forte-fortissimo, forte-fortissimo,
forte-fortissimo, forte-fortissimo, forte-fortissimo,
repeat ad lib,
deve sembrar genuino….

…and, with the hypothetical music which isn't music, which is really just words, marching *forte-fortissimo* in his head, the composer scribbles down *'deve sembrar genuino'* again.

And then again.

And then, to make sure, again.

And then, having reached the bottom of the page, he writes it on his hand.

Then the keyboard of the piano.

Then the legs of the piano, the floor, the walls, the bed—now *forte-fortissimo* shouting out loud, in unison with the *forte-fortissimo* in his head, *'Deve sembrar genuino. Deve sembrar genuino. Deve sembrar genuino.'* But the more desperately he shouts, the more desperately he writes, the less genuine the phrase sounds or looks.

'Deve sembrar genuino. Deve sembrar genuino. Deve sembrar genuino,' he shout-sobs, until the phrase seems the least genuine sound in the world…

…or, that is, until the un-genuine sound of the *forte-fortissimo* knock-crack-knock on the door, the un-genuine sound of a *forte-fortissimo* scuffle, the un-genuine sound of a blacked-out car revving, and its *forte-fortissimo* screaming brakes…

…and later the un-genuine sound of their questions, and of his *forte-fortissimo* screams, long into the morning.

Smiling List

You have to remember: smile, keep smiling, smile, keep smiling, smile, keep smiling, crotchet-crotchet-quaver-quaver, crotchet-crotchet-quaver-quaver...

The Principal Conductor always smiled when he conducted. And he always smiled when he said, 'You have to remember. I am the Principal Conductor now.'

Ted did remember.

'You have to remember. I am the Principal Conductor now.'

Ted did remember. He wasn't allowed to forget.

He'd always sat next to Kaye, ever since the Burslem Philharmonic had been founded, ever since his first wife had died on him, ever since he'd got bored with grief and had decided to scratch his violin again. He and Kaye had been among the founder members, and they'd even assumed the conductor's stick when the real conductors had been busy with other out-of-tune bands.

He never talked to Kaye outside Tuesday evenings, never bumped into her shopping in Hanley, never phoned her about some particularly difficult passage-work. But every Tuesday for years—barring Christmas and annual holidays in Llandudno— he was there, next to her, trying to keep pace with her fingers.

She was leader, he was deputy leader: that was the Burslem tradition.

But three decades and two ex-wives on, he found himself exiled from Kaye and her smile.

'You have to remember. I am the Principal Conductor now,' said the Principal Conductor, as he banished Ted to the second drawer of violins.

'You have to remember. I am the Principal Conductor now,' said the Principal Conductor, as he banished Ted to the third drawer of violins.

'You have to remember...'

'I know,' said Ted, 'you are the Principal Conductor now, and you are banishing me to the Gulag of violins. I'll be playing kazoo if this goes on.'

'I won't have insubordination.'

'I thought this was a democratic orchestra,' said Ted.

'Democracies don't have insubordination,' said the Principal Conductor.

'Kazoo it is then,' said Ted.

Kaye seemed a long way away in his new position at the back of the violins. She was much nearer the Principal Conductor's smile than Ted's.

She was even further away when he was sent to the violas.

'You play viola, don't you, Ted?' asked the Principal Conductor. 'We've only got a couple since Vince left. It'll be a good opportunity for you to brush up an old trick.'

The violas welcomed Ted, but none had Kaye's smile. And if Ted didn't have Kaye's smile any more, nor did he have his own. During a performance of Shostakovich's Ninth Symphony, the Principal Conductor caught him crying.

'Why were you crying during Shostakovich's Ninth

Symphony?' asked the Principal Conductor, who never cried at anything.

'Because it was sad,' said Ted.

'How ridiculous,' said the Principal Conductor, 'it's a light-hearted, jolly-hockey-sticks piece for the end of the war.' He paused. 'And even if it were sad, you shouldn't be sad. An orchestra can't be sad. We're performers—no more, no less than ballerinas. We have to be smiley all the time. You have to smile when you play, whatever you play, because the audience is watching you.'

'Who says?'

'I say, and I'm the Principal Conductor. I want this orchestra to be made of smilers. I want everyone smiley, whatever they're playing, whether it's a funeral march or a festival march, Shostakovich or a Beatles medley. We're here to please the audience, not ourselves, and we should be seen to be enjoying what we play. We should be smilers, not weepers.'

'I see.'

'Yes, you see. And if you don't see, I'm afraid you'll have to be sent to the back drawer of the violas.'

'What if I do see?'

'Then I might think about putting you back in the violins—just a trial period, of course. Just a trial.' He looked narrowly at Ted. 'But I want you to do something for me and the orchestra first. I want you to look around during the next performance. I can't watch everyone while I'm busy conducting. So I want you to take a note of who is smiling and who isn't. I want to know who is a smiler, who a weeper. In short, I want a list; a smiling list.'

'What will you do with the smiling list?'

'I am the Principal Conductor. I will decide what to do with the smiling list.'

At the next concert, the Burslem Philharmonic played a symphony by someone called Kabalevsky which the Principal Conductor had chosen. Ted watched the violists, the violinists, the cellists, the bassoonists, the oboists, the flautists, the harpists, the one-time-friendists, and mentally noted down who didn't smile. He couldn't see Kaye—he could only see the back of her head—but he was sure she was smiling, and (moreover) smiling genuinely.

After the Kabalevsky and the weak applause, the Principal Conductor asked Ted who was on his list. Ted asked if he were going to be promoted back to the violins. The Principal Conductor said yes, probably, probably, yes, he thought so. Ted asked if he was going to be promoted back to the first violins. The Principal Conductor said yes, probably, probably, yes, he thought so. Ted asked if he was going to be promoted back to the front desk—back to Kaye's smile. The Principal Conductor said he would think about it. The Principal Conductor asked Ted again who was on his list of non-smilers.

Ted said, 'No one.'

The Principal Conductor asked: 'No one?'

Ted said, 'No one.'

The Principal Conductor said: 'Watch out, Ted, or you'll be on The List on your own. This is your last chance. Are you sure it was no one?'

Ted told him he was very sure. Ted told him that everyone was smiling—indeed, everyone was laughing because it was a crap piece of music. Ted told him everyone was laughing at the Principal Conductor's taste in symphonies. Ted told him to fuck his Kabalevsky and his smile.

That night, Ted listened to his stereo and shed a few tears for a certain Ninth Symphony by a certain Dmitri Shostakovich.

He thought about how Shostakovich had been put on a list back in the 1940s. Shostakovich hadn't been much of a smiler either.

Ted picked up the phone and dialled Kaye.

Classical Section

'We don't want to pre-empt any kind of breakdown or, you know, drinking problem, do we, Rob?'

'Of course not, Ellie.'

'We—Rob and I—just can't help but be aware that you've been struggling a bit recently.'

'A bit. Not surprising really.'

'Not at all surprising. It can't have been easy for you, what with your mother's ... hands, and all the staff restructuring.'

'Must've been very hard.'

'So we don't want to pre-empt any kind of breakdown or drinking problem.'

'Of course not.'

'We just want you to look after yourself. And you can bank on our help with that. After all, it's our job to look after shop staff.'

'Our job.'

'It's our job to look after you and your sales. We know you've had problems lately, hitting your Strauss and Schubert targets, getting Tchaikovsky off the shelves and out the door.'

'You know the figures.'

'And we know that you feel a little aggrieved being taken off the *M*s to *O*s after so many years. It's our job to make difficult judgement calls, and we thought one of the new faces would suit *M*s to *O*s better.'

'But we don't want any ill-feeling.'

'We don't want you to feel that you're being driven out, gradually replaced by younger faces.'

'That's not what classical music is about, is it, Ellie?'

'Of course not—pop might be, but not the classical section. Down here, you see, it's all about the wisdom of age. A lot of these composer guys didn't write anything worth a clef till they were … way past your age.'

'It's all about golden oldies down here.'

'Yes, and that's why you mustn't feel like you're being elbowed out by younger, and more … energetic colleagues.'

'We don't want you to feel that.'

'We're afraid that you *do* feel like that, but we don't want you to. We understand that you think losing the Mozarts and Mahlers has reduced your sales potential. You've probably grown attached to them after all these years. But you could look at it as an opportunity — you've lost your Mozarts and Mahlers, but you've gained the Schuberts and Schumanns.'

'And that more than makes up for the *X*s, *Y*s and *Z*s, the Xenakises and the Zemlinskys.'

'With a bit of imagination, a bit of sprucing up displays and clever ordering, you might even tempt people to the Zemlinskys. It's a matter of leading their eyes from the Schubert *Unfinisheds* across to the Zemlinsky *Lyric Symphonies*.'

'A bit of imagination, and you might even shift the odd Stockhausen or Schnittke.'

'Well, you never know. The point is that you can make the *S*s to *Z*s your own. Put your own imprint on the displays and ordering, your own individuality. Use your imagination. Think outside the

CD box, as they say. Experiment. You never know what may come of it.'

'Anything is possible, given the will.'

'You never know what may come of it. In a couple of years, you might have done so well with your Ss and Zs, you could work your way up to the Bs, or even the compilation section.'

'Imagine that.'

'Imagine the sales then. All those CDs of busty opera singers and sexy quartets, selling by the hundred.'

'Classic FM charts, here we come.'

'Whatever happens in the future, though, we want you to know that we're supporting you all the way.'

'All the way.'

'We're not the kind of managers who put pressure on people. We wouldn't drive members of staff out, pre-empt breakdowns or drinking problems.'

'Of course not.'

'We're the kind of managers who have the interests of their staff at heart. And I tell you, it's not easy. We sometimes feel like we've got the whole weight of the shop and all the staff problems on our shoulders. It hurts us personally to see a member of our staff unhappy, whether he or she is perhaps drinking a little too much, worrying a little too much, snapping at customers, obviously not sleeping—or whatever the particular case may be.'

'Whatever the case may be, we can feel that you're unhappy, and unhappiness doesn't make for good music sales, does it, Ellie?'

'No, Rob. We can't have unhappiness in the classical music section. Anyway, we hope you understand our position better now. We want you to be happy. We don't want you to feel desperate, or driven to anything you don't want to be driven to. We want you to know that you can talk to us. Come to us with your problems. Our door is open. Our door is always open. It's better to talk these things through than keep them bottled up. That way lies discontent, maybe something worse—like drink or breakdowns, or ... other mental health problems. Look what it did to Tchaikovsky. We don't want Tchaikovskys on our staff. We don't want to see you developing problems like that. Of course not. I mean, you've had such terrible things happen to you recently—what with your mother's hands, your friends leaving, your ... realignment in the shop hierarchy. We want you to know that we know and we understand. We would hardly want you to feel worse. We would hardly want you to be driven to drink or anything.'

'Of course not.'

'Keith, I think this chat has helped a lot. Don't you, Keith? It's made us all understand one another better, hasn't it, Keith? You, me and Rob—we all understand one another now. Thank you for coming in, Keith.'

'Thank you for coming in, Keith.'

'Thank you,' said Keith as he pulled the door behind him. 'Thank you.'

Thank you, he thought, as he walked back to the shop floor. *Thank you*, he thought, as the Mozart on the tannoy replaced his bosses' voices. *Thank you*, he thought ... and ... and a strange memory came back to him—a memory of watching his mother's fingers spinning through a movement of a Mozart piano concerto, while a crackly LP accompanied her from a corner of the room. The fingers were gone, but for the first time since her diagnosis, he felt okay about things. For the first time in two cancerous years, he felt happy. Ellie and Rob would look after him, he was sure. The fingers were gone, but here was Mozart on the tannoy and two kind people who knew how he felt. Who understood.

He thought he might open a bottle of wine that night to

53

celebrate. He'd put the old accompaniment LP on the record player and listen to it without the solo part.

And he'd have a glass of wine.

Just a glass or two.

Kein Töd in Venedig

The ex-composer yawns (atonally) while his own black dots return to swarm round him like unswattable flies.

At the end of his two-minute setting for soprano, prepared piano and taped whale-song, 'The Kraken,' he stands dutifully and nods at the audience, more because he wants to unstick his buttocks from the plastic chair he is sitting on than from any pleasure in the applause or the performance. Here I am, he thinks, inhaling old flies I thought I'd squashed underfoot, and I'm expected to be pleased about it.

The ex-composer re-applies his buttocks to the chair and sighs (atonally)—all that's left now of the conference is a two-hour lecture by an academic who's kindly going to tell him what his two-minute song is about. This is good, he thinks, because he himself hasn't got a fucking clue.

The lecture begins and, within minutes, he's convinced that every sentence simply *must* be the second to last. If someone would nudge her, perhaps they'd precipitate her into the conclusion. Or perhaps if I break eye contact, he thinks, that'll make her stop—otherwise, she's obviously going to insist on addressing all her 'very best' remarks straight at my face for the next two hours, or two minutes, or however long is left.

He looks around the seminar room; all the usual suspects are here, of course—a structuralist, a poststructuralist, a postmodernist, a deconstructionist, a psychoanalyst, a feminist, a feminist-psychoanalyst, a generalized and rather neurotic combination of the above, a writer of a book on Bucks Fizz, a woman concerned about diminished fifths, an Oxbridge 'Kraken' in too small a pool, a cripplingly shy old charlatan in too large a jacket, and a perplexed businessman in the wrong room.

The ex-composer tries once more to attune his hearing to the lecture. It's a common experience, he thinks—when one is really, *really* bored, it becomes almost impossible to assimilate the meaning of complete sentences, and gradually phrases fragment into single words and sounds which, in isolation, seem wonderfully symphonic and impressive, but which are not connected to anything else. The best politicians realize this subliminal symphonism, even if, like Ronald Reagan, it's only with acting, old age and Alzheimer's.

The ex-composer decides to stare nonchalantly out of the window to see if that will put her off. It isn't that he violently disagrees with, or is offended by, this female Reagan of (B-list) academia, and her efforts to find in the song's use of Neapolitan chords 'a symbolic connection between the Kraken's "huge sponges of millennial growth" and his [overweight] Italian mother.' No, what bothers him is the expectation in her gaze that, as 'the composer', he should care at all about a song he wrote two years ago, *before* 2.14 p.m. on 4th May 2000 AD.

Before he'd become an *ex*-composer, stuffed and wooden like the *ex*-parrot in *Monty Python*.

Outside the window is a sham-Oxford quadrangle, which, the composer fondly imagines, might on sunny days be filled with lazy female students lounging on the grass, their breasts pointing towards the sky. Today, it's filled with drizzle and peeling posters announcing 'Rugby First Team perform can-cans from *Moulin Rouge* at The Seven Seals bar tonight.' The ex-composer's gaze travels over these posters, around the quadrangle, and then climbs the opposite wall. The first-floor room is white and empty, apart from a heater and some uprooted street furniture; the second-floor room is...

Oh, my God—she's in there, and she's taking off her ... she's taking off her ... breasts?—no, that's not right—she's taking off her bra. My God. She's taking off her bra.

The ex-composer suddenly realizes his mouth is wide open, and snaps it shut, looking furtively round the seminar room. But no one else has noticed—everyone else is still intent on the fully-clothed Prof. Ronaldetta Reagan and the generalized noises she's making into the mic.

Fucking unbelievable—you silly bastards. There's a young, beautiful woman undressing over there—yes, over there, you blind gits—and you're listening to an incomprehensible lecture about a raspberry I once blew.

He looks back at the girl, who's now standing, with her (beautifully shaped) back to the window, in just her knickers, her thick, dark hair loose over her shoulders. She reminds him somewhat of a stripper he'd seen on his stag night (many, many thousands of years ago) whose stage name was Jezebel, and whose speciality was re-enacting various sections of the Book of Revelations with strobe lighting and a snake called Leviathan. Kissograms had more intellectual substance in those days.

With all his might, he wills the girl to turn round and to slip out of her knickers, agreeing with God to pawn any meagre musical talent he has left in return for one look, one touch, one grope. He so desperately wants to see her breasts in motion, vibrating slightly under his fingers. Perhaps, he thinks, if you had sensitive enough ears, you'd be able to hear the low, murmuring hum made by breasts vibrating everywhere as women jog, walk, sigh, talk. (Perhaps, if you had sensitive enough ears, you'd still be able to hear my wife's breasts vibrating as she stepped into that road; after all, the great inventor Marconi was convinced that past sounds never die, but just get quieter and quieter and quieter and...)

Prof. R. Reagan isn't getting quieter, but is still groaning on incoherently like the teacher in *Charlie Brown*. Noise pollution, he thinks—it's white noise like this that gets in the way of hearing the things that really matter. Why should I care what she has to say? She certainly wouldn't care what I've been doing for the last two years. I haven't written anything she'd recognize as music for that long—since, of course, 2.14 p.m. on 4th May 2000 AD.

Still, the jingles he'd composed for Supernova Chocolate Products Ltd. had been really successful, in their way. He was particularly fond of the ones he'd done for Dog Chocs and a laxative called Chocs Away. The advert for the latter pictured, in close-up, a huge and hairy woman's face, which was all screwed up with strain and discomfort, but which gradually transformed, with a sigh and a plop and some cunning digital image manipulation, into a svelte, relaxed, smiling blonde. The ex-composer had sampled bits of industrial engineering for the constipation, and had then gradually faded this into a synthe-sized version of Beethoven's *Pastoral Symphony*, with added bird song. The studio manager, Geoff Jefferson (studio managers always seemed to be called Geoff) declared it 'a masterpiece'. Indeed, he had even offered the ex-composer a long-term contract if he'd agree to write the 'incidental music' for a Channel 5 soft-porn show called *Cream Crackers*. Geoff reckoned he had the stylistic versatility to cope with the diverse demands made by the many different kinds of shagging to be featured. The ex-composer had graciously declined.

My God, he thinks, thank you, thank you—Jezebel *is* reaching down to take her knickers off. She's turned to face the window, and is going to reveal all to me. It's going to happen. It's...

'...And, since we have him here, let us take the opportunity to ask the composer himself what he thinks of my interpretation of the modulation?'

What? Oh, bugger, Prof. Reagan's asking me a question and everyone's turned to look at me through their beards. 'I ... er ... yes, certainly, I would ... very much agree, or, at least ... to a certain extent and with certain provisos. Yes, indeed.' Shit, I've got no idea what I've just agreed to. Perhaps I should say something else.

Awkward pause, frowns, coughs, quizzical stares. The nostrils of the academic sitting nearby loom disparagingly.

Why should I care — you can all fuck off. I wrote the shite song before 2.14 p.m. on 4th May 2000 AD. Before I didn't hear the ambulance, before I didn't hear my wife crying and bleeding into the tarmac, before I didn't hear the trucker, who was too busy listening to Megadeth, bounce her off his bumper, before I didn't hear her heels clacking away as she was saying she was just popping across the road to buy a Mozart CD for her brother, before I was too busy perving at the sales assistants in *New Look* who were playing 'Dancing Queen' too loud for me to hear anything.

'Yep. That's right ... in a way,' he adds. It doesn't matter. Reagan's ambient noise starts up again and carries on regardless, without need of prompt or response.

He looks back up at the window opposite. Jezebel (damn it) now has on a little flowery dress, seamed stockings and a tiara. For one terrifying, ravishing second, she turns to look out of the window, seemingly straight at the ex-composer, and is then gone, turning off the light and shutting the door behind her.

Never mind. The composer has already decided to see if Geoff Jefferson's offer is still open. He'll never know that his Jezebel isn't actually female at all, but a member of the university's Rugby First Team dragged up to do some can-canning to a drum-and-bass version of Offenbach. And, of course, it doesn't matter in the slightest.

Musica Somni

Your musical snores are keeping me awake again: in-out-in-out-in-out, all to the first few notes, those repeated D naturals, of bloody 'Nessun Dorma'. I admit an aria about no one sleeping might be kind of apt for me lying here, having to listen to you— but, honestly, why can't you be more imaginative in your snoring? If you knew even a bit about opera—if you bothered to listen to my CDs with me, or come to my performances—perhaps your snores wouldn't be so predictable, so bloody repetitive. In fact, if you bothered to take an interest in *my* interests, you might come to understand the different roles—and realize you should leave the tenor arias to me, and be a bit more, well, feminine, a bit more soprano- or alto-ish in your night noises, your rasps, gurgles and whimpers. You could have been my Butterfly, my Mimi, but instead I'm lying next to a snoring Pavarotti:

> *Nessun dorma! Nessun dorma!*
> *Tu pure, o, Principessa,*
> *nella tua fredda stanza,*
> *guardi le stelle*
> *che tremano d'amore,*
> *e di speranza!*

In-out-in-out-in-out: a *crescendo* of rasping, until there's a pause and your breathing stops and everything goes cold ... and then again from the start:

Nessun dorma! Nessun dorma!

No, I won't, can't, sleep with your Puccinian snores in my face. So instead, I'll just have to lie here and listen. And lying here, listening to music—even the 'music' snorting out of your mouth and nose—makes me remember. You know I've always had a musical memory, rather than a common or garden one, and now, in this sleeplessness, your snores snake-charm a memory out of me—a memory of a time which seems at once so recent and so distant....

We were in the Maer Hills—do *you* remember?—rambling down from the trig point and observatory, skirting the edges of mini-cliffs, pushing through rhododendrons, plucking at blueberries round our shins as we passed. I was ahead of you, pretending not to be lost—but we'd never come this far before, and the paths were thin, muddy, complex. The distance between us was increasing, as I strode ahead and you meanderingly moaned behind, about where we were going, were we lost, couldn't we just go back, why didn't I want to get a kitten, it wouldn't be too much hassle, it would learn not to meow when I was rehearsing my songs, I'd grow to love it, we could call it Sylvie or anything I wanted, even something from opera, and it'd be like our baby, a kind of low-maintenance substitute for what I was giving up, when I finally got the divorce from *her*, moved away from my old life, and settled down with you and Sylvie, or whatever the kitten was called, and everything would be full of....

But then I interrupted you by holding up my hand, and pointing—*Hey, look!*—at some rusty railings, overgrown with bracken, half-blocking a black hole in the escarpment in front. 'I wonder what's in there,' I said, and you said, 'Nothing, nothing at all,' and I said, 'I don't believe that,' and you said, 'Let's go home,' and I said, 'Not yet—come on, we've never seen this before,' and you said, 'I don't want to see it now. I want to get a kitten called Sylvie,' and I said, 'Don't be so bloody babyish-timid,' and I bent down and peered through the railings into the blackness, and shouted, 'Don't be so timid' again, listening to the echo downwards.

Don't be so tim-im-id-id-id…

'Let's go home,' you said. 'Come home with me.'

But I was already tearing the broken railings away from the long grass, and kicking them flat, so I could step closer to the cave opening. You came up behind me, put a hand on my shoulder, and bent down and sniffed. 'It smells of wee and pot,' you said, 'there're probably some crims or thugs or hippies down there.'

'No, there aren't,' I said, 'the smell's just in your *Daily Mail* head. It smells of moss, bark and damp. I'm going to take a look down. I bet no one's been down for ages.'

'Don't,' you said.

'Look,' I said, pushing at the roof of the cave's opening, 'it's all perfectly sound. Nothing's going to happen.'

'Don't,' you said.

But I'd already stepped across the cave's threshold. It was easy going: I only had to bend my head, and the path sloped gently downwards.

About twenty yards down, the path forked into two tunnels, diverging into two different kinds of darkness. I glanced back at you, framed in the sunlight behind me.

63

'Don't worry,' I called, 'I'll only be a minute. I just want to take a look.'

'It's too dark without a torch,' you called back.

'I'll use my lighter,' I said, listening to the last word distorted, deepened and dissected by the tunnels' echoes.

Li-igh-ter-ter-er-er...

I took out my lighter, and stepped forward—into the left tunnel, I think it was.

One last time you called: 'Don't go,' and one last time, I answered you: 'Don't worry. I tell you what, I'll sing-hum-whistle so you can hear me. And it'll help me too, to remember the way back. You know I remember things best through music.'

So I sang-hummed-whistled—of all things—'Nessun Dorma', the first aria that came into my head:

> *Ma il mio mistero è chiuso in me,*
> *il nome mio nessun saprà!*
> *No, No! Sulla tua bocca lo dirò*
> *quando la luce splenderà!*

as I took the right tunnel into the darkness, then left, then a few feet forwards, then right—into a dead end—so back again, then left, then slip-sliding down a short scree slope to a narrow archway—then, deciding there was nothing but earth and black- ness and silence down here, and having (I hoped) frightened you a bit out of your complacency, your taking me for granted, your nagging about kittens and divorces—scrambling back up again, and then left—

—or was it right? And then left, and then to a dead end, and then sparking the lighter up again—and then upwards, and then left, and then slip-sliding down that scree slope again to the narrow archway—and then scrambling up again—and then the aria was over and I started again—left again—right again—down again and the lighter went out again and I sparked it up again and the song ended again—and I thought I heard a female chorus in the echoes:

> *Il nome suo nessun saprà,*
> *E noi dovrem, ahimè, morir, morir! ....*

—and I started to sing-hum-whistle the aria again—and you know I've always had a musical memory, rather than a common or garden visual one, so I was certain the music was leading me out of the cave and towards the light. I was sure the music was remembering the way back to you....

And it must have been, because—finally, finally—those repeated D naturals in your snoring bring me back to now, lying by your side in bed ... where I suddenly realize there's another noise in the room, another, second snoring in this sleep-opera, in-out, in-out, in-out, in-out ... and I look down, to the foot of the bed, and see a kitten, not snoring but purring, like a female chorus.

And both your snoring and the kitten's purring *crescendo* to *fortissimo*, and then there's a pause again—and in that suspended moment of cold and breathless silence, I suddenly realize I don't remember when we finally decided to get a kitten, which may or may not be called Sylvie. I realize I don't remember when I finally got the divorce from *her*. I realize I don't remember moving away from my old life, and settling down here, in this home, with you.

I realize I don't know why there is a tear stain on your cheek.

I realize—I realize I don't remember getting out of the cave, all those days or weeks or months or years ago.

Jonathan Taylor

There is a cold and silent space between us.
I reach over to touch your unbreathing mouth.

Ed il mio bacio scioglierà il silenzio che ti fa mia!

You exhale.
I realize—

...but...

I told you I loved you, but...

'Aways a "but".'

...but I couldn't cope any longer with ... with how well you coped.

'I never get this particular "but" of yours.'

...but I couldn't cope with your coping.

'Well,' you said. 'I can't cope with your not coping with my coping.'

...but that's just it, I said. It's impossible. In the night, when I wake you for the fourth time with a bump and a 'help help help,' you cope. In the morning, when you haven't had any sleep and I need toileting, you cope. In the evening, when you've had a nine-to-seven at work and you come home to me, bloody on the floor, surrounded by broken milk bottles, you cope. You always cope.

'How could I possibly cope if I didn't cope?'

...but you shouldn't cope. You should let go. You should shout and cry and punch me. Be like other carers. Push me down the stairs. Eff and blind about the thing that's changed the body you fell in love with. Your coping, it's like an army operation, a Napoleonic battle plan. Everything is done efficiently, to a time-table, without a fuss. I *want* fuss. I *demand* fuss. I *want* you to rage

67

against the dying of the light, against the thing that's snatching my body. Bastard-fucking-shite-fucking-cunt of a body-snatching illness. Say 'bastard-fucking-shite-fucking-cunt' after me.

'No.'

...but you must. Else what's the point? If you can cope with me now, how can you possibly have loved me before now?

'There are times when I don't cope. Honestly.'

But with that, you tucked a serviette in my collar. I took it out and threw it into the soup. It made me so angry—here we were, having a row about not coping, and all the time you were still coping, still sticking to a schedule, still arranging serviettes.

'There are times when I *don't* cope. I don't cope when you're listening to that deafening opera stuff on the stereo. It's horrid, it makes me cry, watching you sitting there, silent, in your own opera world.'

...but I can't do without it. It choreographs the Parkinson's, makes my tremors tremor in time—don't you see? *Die Fledermaus* waltzes my twitching feet, *Madama Butterfly* lullabies my shaky hands, *Aïda* marches my thoughts into order. Levodopa, get stuffed. Opera's the only medicine.

'So that's it, then? The only time I don't cope—when you're listening to that rubbish—is the one time you do?'

...but ...

'That's it, then.'

...but ...

'That's it. If you can't cope with my coping, I'll take it else-where.' And you packed your suitcase, folding every item neatly, leaving my pills in a row on the windowsill, with a schedule next to them: 'Don't forget ...'

...but it's lonely with just Madama Butterfly and me in the flat. To be frank, she doesn't cope very well with things either.

...but ...

...but ...

...but perhaps *un bel dí* you'll come and see how I'm getting on with the pill schedule you left. 'How are you getting on with the pill schedule I left?' you'll ask.

...but you'll already have seen what the answer is. My shakes will be much worse, my cardigan smeared with broccoli that missed my mouth. You'll take me by the arm and we'll shuffle together into the sitting-room. I'll be excited about something, something I want to show you. It'll take me a minute to get the words out properly.

...but eventually I'll manage it, and you'll understand that I want a CD put on. You'll cry, thinking I'm dredging up the old row.

...but I'm not. As Madama Butterfly's *hara-kiri* fills the room, you'll look from me to the stereo, from the stereo to me, and realize something. You'll realize that the music doesn't lullaby me any more. You'll realize that the shakes are now too bad, the face too masked, the drooling too automatic, the disease too far gone for the Japanese geisha to soothe my restlessness into rest.

...and you'll take my shaking hand and let your hand share the shakes. And I'll take your tears and let my eyes share them. And we'll both have this one tiny moment, before the soprano falls on her sword, before the music stops, of not coping together.

'Je Ne Regrette Rien'

13th June 2001

My dearest Maye,

I don't know how to start this letter. I can't ask 'te souviens-tu encore un peu de moi?' because I'm sure (I hope) you couldn't forget me. And there's no point saying how long gone are those dear Piafian evenings, because we both know that.

I could tell you why I'm writing. In the *Evening Sentinel* last night, I saw your sad news—that your Charles had died 'after a long illness'. I'm sorry for you, and would like to send my condolences.

Would like to, but can't. I'm glad the old bugger's gone—'Enfin Le Printemps', I can't help thinking. I know you probably don't want to hear that, but you've always known how I feel. It was a choice between him and me, and you chose the guy who stopped you being Edith Piaf.

You were *la meilleure* Piaf in the whole of Stoke, you did the best 'La Vie en Rose', you looked gorgeous in that black dress—and the old bugger knew it, and stopped you. Just so you could sew up his cardigans and warble over his ironing board. The North Staffordshire Piaf Society—and I speak here in my official capacity as its ex-president and your ex-manager, ex-Louis Leplée—never

70

recovered. Speaking personally for myself, I never did either. It was all his fault.

I know it's a bit soon for me to write like this, and I'm sorry, but I've waited many, many years to hear your Piaf again. And, well, there's another reason why I have to write now; why I can't wait much longer. But we'll talk about that when we meet. I do hope you'll write back.

Sending you all my 'Mots D'Amour',

Jack

My dearest Maye,

I wrote a letter in June, but never sent it. I thought it was a bit soon to get back in touch, a day or so after your husband had died.

No, that's not true. Actually, I forgot to post it. I thought I had posted it, and then forgot I hadn't. I found the letter the other day among a pile of clothes. So I thought I'd try again.

It probably sounds thoughtless, forgetting to post an important letter. I suppose it is, but it's not a thoughtlessness I can help. You see, I keep forgetting things—even important things, like your letter, the dog's name, what I was doing thirty-seven years and 364 days ago when I heard Piaf had died.

But I don't forget the long-ago time when we were 'Les Amants D'Un Jour'. You were my 'Little Sparrow', I was your Marcel Cerdan. But unlike Piaf and Cerdan, it was you who got married to someone else. Two of us adored you, and you chose the one who wouldn't take you to see her grave in Père Lachaise, who couldn't speak French, who didn't know who Baudelaire was, who didn't wear a carnation in his buttonhole—who didn't even *have* a buttonhole. You chose the one who wouldn't drive you a mile down the road to give a farewell concert in Burslem working men's club. I had to stand in front of your audience and say 'Sorry, Ms Piaf hasn't turned up, shall I fill in with my Chevalier?'

But now Charles is dead, and I wonder if we could restage that last concert, three decades late? I could contact the new president of the North Staffs Piaf Society (he's a Sinatranian in his spare time, but he's okay), and get the ball rolling. What do you think? One last comeback, one last 'Je Ne Regrette Rien', for old times' sake?

All my 'Mots D'Amour',

Jack

19th March 2002

My dearest Maye, my Potteries Piaf,

I know I wrote you a letter before, but can't quite remember if I sent it or not. I can't find it in the flat, so perhaps I did. But I didn't get a reply, so perhaps I didn't. My memory isn't what it used to be, as the doctor says.

If you are getting these letters, and you don't want to reply, that's fine. Just throw them out: 'Rien de rien...'

But I would love to hear from you, my 'Little Sparrow'. I would love to hear your Piafian lilt once more. The closest I get to music these days is the dog's wailing when I've forgotten his Pal with Marrowbone.

Sometimes, even the dog's wailing takes me back there, to the old Victoria Hall in '64, and you on stage, all four foot ten of you, warbling 'Les Feuilles Mortes': 'Il dit: "Rappelle-toi tes amours."' We wore black and cried for our dead Little Sparrow—even the trumpeter's notes wobbled—but with you there in front of us, it seemed like she'd come back to bless us one last time. If Presley can do it, why not Piaf?

That was the greatest moment of the North Staffs Piafs, the pinnacle. Those were the days, my dear. Nothing was ever the same again after that final wink you gave us in the stalls.

'Mots D'Amour',

Jack

16th November 2002

Dearest Maye,

One day I'll want to send you one of these letters. One day I'll remember.

My memory's much worse. I get to the end of sentences and can't remember where I started off from. So getting to the end of a whole letter might be hard. But I'll try.

I found this (enclosed) and wanted to send it to you. It's an old cutting from the *Evening Sentinel*, a review of that concert in the Victoria Hall—a lovely photo of you with your black dress, wig, pencil eyebrows, standing in front of the old mic we used.

How is Charles? Still the uncouth, cardiganed old bugger we Piafians loved to hate? Him and his Mantovani.

Anyway, I hope you'll write back soon. 'If you love me, really love me, let it happen.' It seems only yesterday you were in that newspaper picture. But then, my memory makes everything seem only yesterday. Even today.

Mots, etc.,

Jack

May [?], 2003

My dearest Little Sparrow, my Piaf,

The dog died yesterday, or last week. I was a bit upset, to be honest—I couldn't remember the old mutt's name when I was trying to bury it in the back yard.

Don't have much company of the doggy or human variety now. Stoke feels like a 'ville inconnue'. The Piafians come round once a week, I think, or send a card, or something. But that's all.

I wonder what you're doing now. I found an old cutting (enclosed) from the *Evening Sentinel*, among some rubbish old letters. It's a picture of you winking in a hall. Can't quite recognize where it is. But it's beautiful.

The dog's died. Buried it with the azaleas it used to eat. Thought it might be happy there. Wanted to say something respectful, but couldn't remember the old bugger's name. Charles or something.

Mots,
Jack

20th December 2003

Dear Maye,

I asked the old bag from Social Services what the date was—that's why the date on the top of this letter is in a woman's hand. Wouldn't want you to think—well, you know.

There never were any other 'you knows', you know. You were the only 'you know'.

News? Well, the dog died some time. I missed a documentary on TV about Piaf in the US. Stuff about her and Cerdan.

Not much Piaf on TV in general.

People don't remember her in Stoke.

She gave a lovely concert in the Victoria Hall once.

More than you could say for the old bag from the SS.

A bientôt,

Jack

Enfin Le Printemps [2004]

Dearest Maye,

Loved the concert the other night. Wonderful; no one winks like you. Told that old bag who comes in to steal my money about it. She said, 'What concert?' They're trying to get at me. Bastards, Mantovani fans the lot of them.

But I won't let them.

I won't.

Je vois s'entrebattre des gestes

Toute la comédie des amours

Sur cet air qui va toujours.

Or something like that.

The dog died. Hated him anyway. Wailed at night.

Jack

[August 2004]

Dearest Maye,

I wanted to tell you. I wanted to tell you that. I wanted to tell you that they've stolen the record of you. The one of the concert. Have you got another?

I wanted to tell you that.

The dog has died.

Old bugger Charles is dead too. In the azaleas. Used to eat them.

No record of you.

Jack

Les Feuilles Mortes [2004]

Dearest Maye,
C'est payé, balayé, oublié
   Je me fous du passé...
   Non, je ne regrette...
   Dog.
   Charles?
   Jack.

Dear Sparrow,
I wanted
   I want
   I wink
   I…
   Azaleas.

A Rondo in Letters

8, Kelsey Drive,
Stoke-on-Trent,
Staffs,
28th March 2004

Dear 'Dad',

Please can you stop sending the box-sets of Bach et al. to our Gary? I know it's you who's sending them. And he doesn't want them any more than I did when I was three—or whatever—years old.

    Alan.

Flat 73a,
Seebald Towers,
London
30th March 2004

Dear Alan,

Sorry, I just thought he might enjoy them. These first two or three years are vital if he's going to be a Bach or Mozart when he's older. I mean, by Gary's age, Mozart was already playing the 'clavier'. By the age of five, you know, he'd composed his first music—the Andante in C and other stuff. So you'll need to work fast with Gary if he's going to keep up. It's now or never that the right hemisphere of the brain—the musical side—needs feeding with Bach, Mozart and Beethoven, so it's not overtaken by the stupidly conventional left side. I read about it the other day in a magazine article called 'How child prodigies are made, not born'. It said that sometimes infantile meningitis can help retard the growth of the left side in favour of the right. Of course, it goes without saying that no one would wish that on anyone, even if child prodigy-ness is the result. But you have to look on the bright (or should I say 'right'?) side of these things, don't you?

    Best wishes,

    Dad

8, Kelsey Drive,
Stoke-on-Trent,
Staffs
7th August 2004

Dear 'Dad',

I've already asked you to stop sending these damned box-sets—and what do you go and send for Gary's third birthday? For Christ's sake, other grandfathers give their grandkids teddies or sweets or cash, but Gary gets the 'Complete String Quartets of Dmitri Shostakovich'. For Christ's sake, Dad, for Christ's sake: what's he going to do with them? Chew them? Are Dmitri Shostakovich's bloody string quartets as tasty as turkey dinosaurs?

Another question: have you been to the doctor recently?

Alan

Flat 73a,
Seebald Towers,
London
9th August 2004

Dear Alan,

Sorry—I seem to have miscalculated again. Honestly, it was with all the right intentions. I was just thinking that, well, unless Gary becomes a prodigy soon-ish, how can he expect to produce enough to compete with your Bachs, Mozarts and the rest? You'll have seen the quantities I'm talking about in the box-sets I've sent. I've been spending the last few months looking into it, doing some sums, and I tell you, some of it beggars belief—Bach wrote over 160 CDs of music in his 65 years, during which time he also fathered 20 children, and married twice. That's roughly 2.462 CDs of music, 0.3 children and 0.0307 wives a year, if you count from age zero. All of which is more than you or me, Alan—but it's not yet beyond our Gary. Not yet.

Think how hard it's going to be for him, though, unless he gets up to speed: unlike our non-existent works, Bach's are published in a 65-volume edition, which would take two musical copyists at normal speed 30 years apiece just to copy out. I bet you didn't realize that? There are 1,126 works listed in Bach's 'BWV' catalogue, plus over 146 works which are probably not by him but might be. Then it's reckoned that he probably wrote another 1,000 works on top of these that have been lost. Idiots. Anyone stupid enough to lose music by J.S. Bach should have their hands cut off … well, something horrid should happen to them anyway.

Personally, I'd say the same on behalf of Schubert. Did you know that his scores were 'recycled' by idiot publishers after his death? Nevertheless, over 998 songs, symphonies and sonatas survive him, which I've calculated means that, during his 31 years of poverty, depression and syphilis, he produced 32.193 master-pieces a year. In that rate of production, he trumps even Mozart, who wrote over 626 compositions in his 35 years, averaging 17.886 a year; and he really did start writing from almost zero years old. That's roughly 14.307 works less than Schubert per annum. Final score from Vienna: Mozart 17.886, Schubert 32.193. Still, you could hardly accuse Mozart of slacking, could you?

Papa Haydn wasn't slacking either when he wrote his twenty or so concertos, 83 string quartets and 104 symphonies. Gosh, I worked out that's 1.351 symphonies a year—or, if you count only the 34 years he was writing symphonies, it's 3.06 a year, a quarter a symphony per month, 0.0085 of a symphony every day.

What do we do every day by comparison? I barely manage to feed the fish, read a magazine, make the tea and practise my mental arithmetic. One magazine I was reading the other day told me that if I carry on with the sums, it'll pay off because I won't get dementia… Problem is, I sometimes think a bit of forgetting wouldn't do me any harm. Perhaps it wouldn't do either of us any harm.

Best wishes,

Dad

Dear 'Dad',

Now you've stopped sending us the box-sets, please, please, please-to-the-power-ten can you also stop sending us these endless lists of calculations about long-dead composers? Gary can't read them, and frankly I can't be bothered.

Have you been to see the doctor yet?

Alan

Flat 73a,
Seebald Towers,
London
21st November 2004

Dear Alan,

But you've got it wrong—they're not just calculations about 'long-dead' composers. I did some more number-crunching, and lots of modern musicians have been as prolific as Haydn et al. Look at Shostakovich, Darius Milhaud and Heitor Villa-Lobos. Look at Gustav Mahler: a hundred years after Haydn, and stupid people might say he was lazy, only writing nine symphonies (if you don't count *Das Lied von der Erde*, and the unfinished Tenth). But people who say that are missing the point: Mahler's symphonies are much longer and he's juggling over 100 instrumentalists at once.

I spent the other day going through his scores, counting the notes. I worked out that he averages about 75 notes (not including rests or other notations) per bar of an orchestral score. That's approximately 135,225 per symphony, 1,217,025 over the nine symphonies. That means he wrote 66.641 notes every day of his life. Yes, it's fewer than Bach, but it's still not bad for someone who was conducting the Vienna Opera at the same time.

If you were to listen to Mahler's 1,217,025 notes, Haydn's 104 symphonies, Mozart's complete works, Schubert's complete works and Bach's complete works end to end, I've calculated it would take you around 612 hours and 45 minutes. This is a very approximate calculation, but it means that you could do it in 25½ days if you didn't sleep. I'd like to try it some time, when I have 25½ days free of feeding the fish, making the tea and doing sums. These days, the sums seem to take up more and more of my time.

When you were three years young, it would never have crossed my mind to listen to 25½ days of music. I wasn't into all this classical stuff back then, unlike your mother. You know, she used to play the piano all the time, particularly Mozart's sonatas, fantasias and rondos. You were too young to remember. Still, there's no point getting all misty-eyed and Tchaikovsky-ish about these things. When I listen to real pianists like Alfred Brendel, I can tell she wasn't very good, poor old girl.

Back then, of course, I wouldn't have known good from bad. I just wanted her to shut her Mozart up. But you change when you get older—I hope you do, anyway—and since she died I've amassed quite a CD collection. It's much bigger than when you last saw it, metres long. The internet's to blame. Online, you can buy, say, the box-set of Beethoven's Complete Works for a snip at £139.99. It's amazing: all you have to do is fill in your credit card number and delivery address, press 'order', and four mornings later a new box-set arrives. I unwrap it and put it in pride of place next to the other great composers on the living-room shelves. You remember the ones—they used to have our photos on them. Now Beethoven takes up 14cm × 12cm × 40cm of the shelves, Mozart 14cm × 12cm × 45cm, but Bach dwarfs them all size-wise because he is 14cm × 12cm × an impressive 55cm.

At the moment, I can't quite bring myself to take down any of these composers and actually listen to them—or, at least, not for more than, say, ten minutes and one second a day. It takes a long time to listen to 45cm of music in snatches of ten minutes and one second—it's the equivalent of only 0.0491cm per day.

Ten minutes and one second ... you know, conveniently enough, that's the precise length of Mozart's Rondo in A minor (K511) when played by pianist Alfred Brendel in my box-set of Mozart's Complete Works for Solo Piano. So I can listen to that piece over and over again. When it comes to a Mahler epic, though, the ten-minutes-and-one-second rule makes things rather tricky. You kind of lose your thread when you return to one of his symphonies 24 hours later, in the middle of some apocalypse or other. How did we get here, I keep wondering, how did we reach this point?

Sometimes, I rewind the CD slightly—perhaps by one minute and thirty seconds—to lead into the apocalypse, so I can hear how the music built up to it. But then I can't make out where that bit comes from either, and I press 'rewind' again. And then again. Eventually, I end up recapping the whole ten minutes and one second that I listened to the previous day, and I get nowhere. I tell you, at times like these, I feel as if I'm doomed to keep listening to those same ten minutes and one second on a loop, never reaching the final chord, never reaching the Resurrection at the end of the Resurrection Symphony, 69 minutes and 20 seconds later. God, Resurrections don't half take a long time.

I think Bach probably felt the same too. Everyone thinks he's so religious, but Bach never reaches the Resurrection either. I've been thinking about this a lot recently, Alan: the *St Matthew Passion* is all about Jesus's suffering, and doesn't get round to the Resurrection bit. When I first listened to it, in ten-minute-and-one-second snippets, I kept expecting the Resurrection to turn up, but it never did. By the third CD, I started thinking Bach was cutting it a bit fine. And then it just ended with 'We sit down in tears,' and no one seemed to have got anywhere, and all Christ had achieved was a lot of whipping for his pains. Bit sadistic, if you ask me.

Best wishes,
Dad

Dear 'Dad',

In one of your last letters, you used the word 'sadistic' about something or someone, can't remember what or who. Look, Dad, I'm sorry to have to say this, but I can't help thinking the word could be applied to you sometimes. Honestly, what you did to our Gary at Christmas was pushy to the point of sadism. It's the same old story, isn't it? Round and round the garden we go: after everything that's been said and done between you and me, you seem determined to repeat it all with our Gary. Leave the kid alone, for Christ's sake. If he doesn't want to produce piano concertos at the age of three—if he'd rather play with his bloody toy cars—well, let him.

There's only one way out here: unless you get round to the doctor sharp-ish, I don't think we can have you visiting for a while, upsetting him like that. I think it'd be best for us to have a rest from each other and, to be frank, from your bloody Mozart sums.

Alan

Flat 73a,
Seebald Towers,
London
31st December 2004

Dear Alan,

I received your letter 25½ hours ago, and have since had four (yes, four) ten-minute-and-one-second sessions of Stravinsky's *Rite of Spring*. It was only when I got to 'The Sacrificial Dance' that I felt a bit better and able to reply.

I'm sorry I was 'sadistic' in buying a £1,245 piano for my grandson's Christmas present. Things seemed to get all mixed up when I was visiting, especially from about 9.34 a.m. on Christmas Eve, when the removal men came to deliver the present. It was their fault, really: they rang the doorbell and, when you answered the door, they didn't explain who they were, so you didn't get the chance to understand what was happening. You were just faced with two Laurel and Hardys (as I call them) trying to squeeze an upright piano into your hallway. They kept banging the piano against the door frame, the piano kept clanging like a gong, you were shouting at them that they'd delivered it to the wrong address, I was shouting at you, trying to tell you that it was the right address, and even little Gary was joining in, holding his hands over his ears and wailing. This wasn't how I'd planned the piano surprise at all.

Jonathan Taylor

When the Laurel and Hardys had finally heaved the piano into the living-room, smashing cacti and ripping wallpaper, I tried to explain calmly that it wasn't the wrong address—that it was a present for Gary from me. You asked me if I was serious, I said yes, and that was when you first called me 'pushy and obsessive and sadistic'. Gary had taken his hands off his ears, and started jumping round the room shouting, 'Saddyistic! Saddyistic! Saddyistic Grandpa!' I know you know what happened—I'm just trying to get it all straight in my head.

And look, I'm sorry for being 'saddyistic'. I hadn't meant it to happen that way. Everything just got confused and the piano was a lead balloon. Because of that, I bet you've never sat him at the keyboard to give him a chance at prodigy-ness. When you were young, I tried to give you a chance, plumping you on the piano stool over and over again—at least (I reckon) 260,000 times over nine years. You kept crawling or jumping or toppling off it, and I kept putting you back on, guiding your little fingers to the keys. It was hard work, and all I got for my pains was being called 'sadistic' and zero symphonies. If you were Haydn, you'd have produced an average of 33.775 symphonies by now. But you know, don't you, that I don't hold that against you? And, well, at least you've produced a Gary.

I hope you will forgive a 'saddyistic' grandpa, and that we will all see each other soon.

Best wishes,

Dad

Grimmet & Timms,
Solicitors (est. 1796),
Terrence Row,
Staffordshire
3rd March 2008

FAO Mr Alan Forster,
8, Kelsey Drive,
Stoke-on-Trent

Dear Mr Forster,

RE ITEMS RECOVERED FROM 73A
SEEBALD TOWERS

Further to our correspondence concerning the sale of your late father's remaining property, the executor has advised me that the CD collection, hi-fi and piano (complete with stool) have now been sold at auction for a total of £145.30. A cheque from the executor is enclosed as well as receipts of sale. Also enclosed is a letter from your father, addressed to you and dated 18th July 2007, which was clearly never delivered. It was discovered by the purchaser of the piano, taped under the lid.

Please can you acknowledge receipt of the cheque and the enclosed documents?

Yours faithfully,

MG Grimmet

Enc.

Dear Alan,

I haven't heard from you in, well, a while. I hope after this time I'm no longer 'Sadistic Grandpa'. I've been good, Alan, honestly: I've been to the doctor, and remembered not to send Gary CD box-sets, mathematical calculations or pianos. Problem is, that means I've run out of things I can think of doing for him.

Perhaps there's one thing I can do, though, which is something I never did when you were a kid: I could tell Gary a story. It's a story the doctor told me, about a 'Sadistic Father' (not Grandfather this time).

This Sadistic Father's wife died when his son was three years, 11 months and six days old. Sadistic Father was sad because he had loved his wife, even if he hadn't loved her piano-playing. His son carried on laughing, crying and, well, pooing regardless—roughly 2.6 times a day.

The son also started climbing onto the piano stool—where Sadistic Father's wife had sat not so long ago—and thumping forwards onto the keys. Sometimes, the son would glissando his toy cars up and down the 88 keys, up and down, down and up, chipping the ivorine. Sometimes, he'd head-butt the keys and burst

97

out screaming. Sometimes, he'd punch as many keys as his little hands could manage, over and over again, in heaps of discords. 'Stop!' Sadistic Father kept shouting. 'Stopstopstopstopstopstop-forchrist'ssakestop!' But the discords wouldn't stop, and the 'stops' themselves became part of the discords, and weeks and weeks went by in a Rondo-without-variation of discords and 'stops' and toy-car-glissandi and head-buttings...

...until the Sadistic Father felt like he was being buried alive in childish dissonance...

...until one day Sadistic Father found himself running into the living-room where his son was pummelling discords, and grabbing his son's tiny wrists with one of his hands and pinning them to the keyboard and slamming down the wooden lid of the piano onto the podgy fingers...

... and he was going to do it again—and again—and again. But then, halfway through doing it again, the lid poised just above his son's fingers, Sadistic Father stopped—and something in his brain rewound to sixteen seconds before.

Sixteen seconds before, he'd been in the kitchen, crying and burning crumpets. The connecting door with the living-room was open, and all he could hear in the world were his son's dissonances. He'd nipped himself with a knife and looked up.

At that precise micro-second—before he stormed into the living-room, before he smashed his son's fingers, before the piano took its revenge for months of abuse—he'd heard something he didn't absorb, didn't register till sixteen seconds later, sixteen seconds too late. Only then did his mind rewind and he recovered something precious hidden among the discordant rubble. Only then did he hear five tiny notes stolen from another world, the world of Mozart's Rondo in A minor, distilled into that five-note chromatic turn with which it starts: E, F natural, E, D sharp, E.

He hadn't noticed the Mozart turn the first time round, when he'd found himself running into the living-room and grabbing his son's tiny wrists with one of his hands and pinning them to the keys and slamming down the lid of the piano onto the podgy fingers. Only afterwards did the scene replay itself in his head, and he picked out the Mozart among the din, the crying, and the broken bones.

It was all he could think of at the hospital—where they believed his story about the piano lid falling onto his son's fingers accidentally. It was all he could think about when they came home, his son in plaster and bandages. It was all he could think about for months, years, afterwards, when he tried to sit his son at the piano stool, tried to induce him to repeat the Mozart turn, perhaps develop it into a whole Rondo. It was all he could think about: his son's early piano abuse might have been a prelude to Mozartian genius. But his son never repeated the chromatic turn, and—although later he didn't seem to remember what his father had done—didn't like the piano any more, didn't want to go near it. So the Rondo theme never came back.

Gary, Alan, after the doctor told me this story, he said that the Sadistic Father was sorry.

With love,

'Dad' and 'Grandpa'

8, Kelsey Drive,
Stoke-on-Trent,
Staffs
5th March 2008

MG Grimmet,
Grimmet & Timms, Solicitors,
Terrence Row,
Staffs

Dear Mr Grimmet,

RE YOUR LETTER OF 3RD MARCH 2008

As requested, I hereby acknowledge receipt of your letter of 3rd March 2008, plus the enclosures—i.e. cheque and receipts from the executor, and the letter (dated 18th July 2007) from my father.

Yours faithfully,

Alan Forster

Introduction and Allegro

It was some piece of music—I could never remember its name.
Back then, when I was a kid, I used to think somehow it sounded
like the cathedral he made with his fingers. You see, whenever
he listened to whatever-it-was, his fingers'd form that cathedral
against his forehead—that huge forehead that went on and on
and never ended in hair—and he'd look a bit like the photo on a
record sleeve, one of his favourites, Jon Sibbellos ... or something
like that.

To be honest, I could never really remember the names of all
those composers. I mean, I never had much time to look at the
labels before the music started, and if I tried looking while the
records were on, I'd just get dizzy and fall down. And my God,
then there'd be hell to pay. No: Father'd just hand me the album
he wanted to hear, and I'd put it on without saying a word, let
alone looking what it was. Then he'd sit like Sibbellos for the
whole piece, and it'd get cold around him.

My job was to change the 78s, because the auto-stacking had
broken a long time ago. I was an expert at it, so quick you'd hardly
notice the joins: slip the first record out of its brown sleeve
and onto the old Victrola, click on ... click off, flip record over,
click on ... click off, slide up, slip next record out of sleeve and

onto the Victrola, click on, slip previous record into sleeve ... and so on and on and on, till it was as cold and dark as shellac. I'd stand there for hours, shifting my weight from foot to foot, a dozen 12-inch 78s poised, desperate not to let the pauses between the five-minute sides get too long—'too long' being more than a couple of seconds. When a couple of seconds happened, Father'd lose his concentration, his cathedralled fingers'd come apart, and that forehead would turn—slowly, slowly—in my direction.

What a bastard he was, my brother says now, treating his seven-year-old daughter like an auto-stacker, just because he was too cheap to buy a new one. What a bastard, making her stand for hours at a time for his selfish-bastardly-snobby pleasure. 'Classics for Pleasure' my arse, my brother says. More like 'Classics for Pain, Classics for Fucking Sadism'.

Bastard, my brother says, a selfish-bastard-snob through and through; nothing more, nothing less. He was a selfish bastard when he was summoned for a tea he didn't want, when he wasn't summoned for a tea he *did* want, when it was sunshiny and he wanted to stay indoors with his 78s, when it was rainy and he *had* to stay indoors with the 78s.

It's so many years ago, I say. There were some okay times, you know.

Bastard, my brother says: don't you go getting all Chikovskee-ish-sentimental on me (or something like that). You have to be strong and remember that there were *only* the bastardly times. Being strong is remembering that, never letting go of it. He hit you, don't you remember? There was that day when I thought he was going to knock your head through the floorboards—all accompanied by sodding Brahms. Just because you'd dropped one of his precious records, there was blood and shellac everywhere. You should've remembered that at his funeral, before you started blubbing. Why did you blub at his funeral? What a waste of tears.

Yes, he was an out-and-out bastard, my brother says. He used you like a machine, like a machine-servant. He used us both worse than servants. Servants—a butler and a maid—in a sodding Hackney flat to an old socialist. He still thought he was at some posh council do in Worcestershire, not on incapacity benefit in North London. I tell you, before the old bastard died, the only thing he could say to me was that he wanted to be 'back 'ome in Worcestershire', and that it was our fault he wasn't. He'd left the council and Labour, come to Hackney to feed his family, got fucked in the legs trying to do it, and look how his kids repaid him. Dropping records, bleeding into floorboards, decades of maliciously cooking him teas he didn't want. Served the bastard right that the cancer more or less ate him to death in the end—the world eating him back. Poetic justice, that's what I say.

Bastard, my brother says.

Bastard, my brother says. Then he asks: will you turn the radio station over again?

As I leave my brother's flat at 7.30 p.m. as I have done every Saturday for ten years; as I wander down Hackney High Street; as I walk back to my council flat; as I pass a Radio Rentals shop front, where someone has left one of the televisions flickering in the dark, I catch some piece of music coming through the window, and I come to a dead stop.

It's that piece of music that sounded like my father's mind. The one that he cathedralled his fingers to. It's accompanied on the TV by a film of a man with a moustache cycling through green and pleasant places—or, at least, grey, pleasant places, because the film is black-and-white.

It ends, and someone on the TV tells me the piece of music was Sir Edward Elgar's Introduction and Allegro for strings. The greeny-grey pictures on the screen, the man tells me, were Elgar's home in the Malvern Hills.

And I wander back to my home, and I think, yes, our father was a bastard.

But not all the time. Not all times were bastardly times. He wasn't a bastard while his eyes were closed and his fingers cathedralled. He wasn't a bastard while his eyes seemed to move from side to side under their lids in time to the music. He wasn't a bastard when I got the records in the right order and didn't drop them. He wasn't a bastard while I kept the Elgar going. He wasn't a bastard when I started the piece all over again, when the Allegro became the Introduction, the Introduction the Allegro, and the Allegro the Introduction, over and over again, to stop the cathedral coming apart, his eyes opening.

And now, in my mind's ear, I just have to keep the Elgar going on forever and ever for it always to be a darkening afternoon at home, my father sitting there with his eyes closed and fingers cathedralled, and for him never to be a bastard, for him never to hurt me with the floorboards again.

And ... and I wonder if, next Saturday evening, there might be any vacancies in a B&B in greeny-grey and pleasant places, somewhere near Malvern.

Synaesthetic Schmidt

Since he had been a young man, Schmidt had listened in colours. Black was silence, brown was a Russian bass, blue was an Italian tenor, orange was his first Elisabeth Schwarzkopf concert, yellow was Herbert von Karajan's conducting, red was … well, red was something else.

For years, he'd told doctors and psychiatrists and neurologists that Bliss's *Colour Symphony* really was in glorious Technicolor, that Gershwin's *Rhapsody in Blue* was actually more of a magenta–mauve hybrid, and that Scriabin's *Prometheus* didn't need the light organ, because it was already there, in front of his eyes. Best of all, Bach's *Art of Fugue* was a counterpoint of rainbows. That's how it had been since the '40s, when he had first heard the *Art of Fugue* arranged for a rather scratchy orchestra.

Of course, none of the doctors had believed him—they'd been interested in other kinds of diagnoses and experiments back then. Fifty years later, though, the medics and scientists were fascinated, and wanted to put him through all sorts of neuro-imaging tests. Was it genetic or adventitious synaesthesia, they wondered? Was it caused by undetected temporal lobe epilepsy in his youth? Was it narrow-band or broadband synaesthesia, or a mixture of both?

But it was too late for these questions and tests, and Schmidt knew it. His glory days of hearing Mozart as refracted light were gone. One day, he'd woken up to hear a screaming, whistling sound in his left ear, as a progressive tinnitus started dyeing the world red.

'What are you hearing?' the GP asked.

'Red,' Schmidt said.

'But how would you describe the sound?' the GP asked.

'Red,' he said.

'But what kind of note is it?'

'Red,' he said, looking around. Everything was red—the GP, the GP's notes, the sky outside the GP's window—everything. Everything was dyed red by a shrill C sharp above the stave.

'We can't find anything, Herr Schmidt, in our tests. There are no apparent causes, no ear infections, no foreign objects in the canal, no related nose allergies. You do not seem to have a low level of serotonin, you do not regularly take aspirin or quinidine—the sorts of things which sometimes cause ringing in the ears. Without a cause, there is nothing we can do, unless... unless you can think of a cause, Herr Schmidt?'

But no, Schmidt couldn't think of a cause.

Schmidt couldn't think of a reason why he would spend his last few years in a red world, under a red sun, with a red wife crying tears reddened by the never-ending dissonance of a C sharp above the stave. He couldn't think of a reason for all this.

He couldn't think of a time when, as a young man, he'd first heard the colour red.

He couldn't think of a time when, as a young officer, he'd listened to a scratchy orchestra playing outside a huge factory; a factory in which he'd spent no more than a few days, before being drafted elsewhere; a factory where he'd tried not to be part of anything, tried to keep his distance, tried and for the most part succeeded—well, except for one minor incident, one long-forgotten moment, when a flautist from the orchestra had needed shooting, and he'd not been able to think of an excuse in time, and he'd heard her last C sharp and then seen the earth and air dyed red round her, and he couldn't—wouldn't—think about it any more.

No, he wouldn't—couldn't—think of that time when Strauss tasted of raining ash, when ash smelt of Léhar, when shoes felt like dead waltzes, when barbed wire looked like a Wagnerian prelude—and when symphonies were ash, shoes, barbed wire, tears, blood.

Acknowledgements

The book's epigraph is taken from Dmitri Shostakovich, *Testimony: The Memoirs of Dmitri Shostakovich As Related to and Edited by Solomon Volkov*, trans. Antonia W. Bouis (London: Hamish Hamilton, 1979), p. 140. Copyright © Solomon Volkov, 1979. Reproduced by permission of Penguin Books Ltd. Also: brief quote from p.140 from *Testimony: The Memoirs of Dmitri Shostakovich* by Solomon E. Volkov. Copyright ©1979 by Solomon Volkov. English language translation copyright © 1979 by HarperCollins Publishers. Foreword © 2004 by Vladimir Ashkenazy. Reprinted by permission of HarperCollins Publishers.

The epigraph to 'Must Sound Genuine' is quoted in Alexander Werth, *Musical Uproar in Moscow* (London: Turnstile, 1949), p. 29.

Thanks are due to Suman Chakraborty; Will Buckingham, Simon Perril, Kathleen Bell and Phil Cox; Vanessa Gebbie; Simon King; the editors of the magazines in which these stories were previously published; my mother, father, Robin, Anna, Sam, Naomi, Erin, Karen, Bruce, Finola, Tancred, Helen, Ben, Dylan; and, of course, Maria, Miranda and Rosalind.

About the Author

Jonathan Taylor is author of the novel *Entertaining Strangers* (Salt, 2012), the memoir *Take Me Home: Parkinson's, My Father, Myself* (Granta Books, 2007) and the poetry collection, *Musicolepsy* (Shoestring Press, 2013). He is editor of the anthology *Overheard: Stories to Read Aloud* (Salt, 2012), winner of the Saboteur Award for Best Fiction Anthology 2013. He is Lecturer in Creative Writing at the University of Leicester in the UK, and co-director of small publisher and arts organization Crystal Clear Creators (www. crystalclearcreators.org.uk). Born and raised in Stoke-on-Trent, he now lives in Leicestershire with his wife, the poet Maria Taylor, and their twin daughters, Miranda and Rosalind. His website is www.jonathanptaylor.co.uk.